SINCERELY,

L.A. BRIEN

Sincerely,

Visit our website at

www.StillwaterPress.com

for more information.
First Stillwater River Publications
Edition
ISBN: 978-1-952521-93-5

1 2 3 4 5 6 7 8 9 10
Written by L.A. Brien
Published by Stillwater River
Publications,

Pawtucket, RI, USA.

Dedication

This book is dedicated to my late father, Johnny O. You have always been my strength, my best friend, and the one person who could make me laugh until I cried. This book is for you Pop, love you always.

Acknowledgements

I would like to thank one of my closest friends who has been such an amazing support system through and through, thank you Barbara Demaio for encouraging me to continue writing. Thank you Scott Lepizzera, words cannot express my gratitude for your support, I am thankful to have you in my life, I love you for being you! Lacey Beaudoin, I owe you the biggest thanks, you helped make this happen. Thank you for being my first reader and helping me to edit. I'm happy to have gone through this journey together, may the next book bring just as many laughs as we had working on this one! Thank you Stillwater River Publications for helping me publish my first book! To my friend Marianne, we have been friends since we were eight years old! I could not have picked a better partner in crime for this story! Thank you for all of your support during this crazy process! Lastly, Ed, I did it! ☺

Prologue

Lou was a self-employed private investigator who ran her own business in Texas. Originally from Pawtucket, Rhode Island, her given name was Lisa, but even her relatives rarely used it.. Her father Michael was the chief of the Pawtucket Police Department, and the last thing he ever wanted was for his daughter to follow in his footsteps.

Michael knew what it took to be in law enforcement. One line her father perpetually threw at her was, "You, my dear…have two of *the worst* qualities for a person in law enforcement: you have no fear and a big heart. It's a deadly combination and it *will* get you killed."

Despite her father's warnings she still became a private investigator. Her family was under the impression that she only investigated cheating spouses. Simple, never really too messy or dangerous. She did…at times; she would refer to that as quick cash. What her family did not know was that her expertise had expanded over the years; she worked with a wide network of police departments on cold cases.

Her parents divorced when she was four years old and her mother Nancy had custody of the three children. Her brother Shane was the oldest, Lou was the middle, and Johnna was the youngest. Johnna was especially close to her; she was the one who gave Lou her nickname. Johnna, from the time she could speak, always called her Lou.

Nancy eventually married a wonderful man named Ronnie who owned a radiator and air conditioner shop in Cumberland. Ronnie had two children, Dave and Deb. Growing up together the five children all got along for the most part, just an occasional argument among siblings here and there, but they always remained close.

Lou had three close friends from childhood as well: Marianne, Bella, and Joanne. Marianne was the funny one in the group. She was five feet, three inches tall with black wavy hair and big brown eyes. She was also the fashionista of the group. She loved music, especially the Beatles, and her second love was horror movies. Lou and Marianne would go to see every horror movie that came out, and if they couldn't see it on the big screen, they would rent it and watch it together. Marianne's fashion sense came in handy as an adult when she opened one of the largest resale shops in Rhode Island.

Bella was the chef; she was five feet, five inches tall and had blond shoulder length hair and brown eyes. As a girl, Bella would always have her friends over and create meals for them to try. Usually they were amazing, but sometimes the girls had to be honest and look at Bella and say, "Not your best work!" or Marianne would tell Bella, "I'd rather have a peanut butter and jelly sandwich!" To no one's surprise, as an adult she opened a very successful catering business.

Now Joanne was the brains of the group. She was five feet, one inch tall with brown hair she always wore short. Joanne always made high honors in school and would often help her friends out with homework. If they wanted to be naughty and bunk school, Joanne would be the one to write the bogus parent notes to excuse them. She graduated college as a doctor of internal medicine. She and her husband eventually moved to Tennessee to start her practice, but the four friends stayed in touch.

Lou considered her friends part of her family. She would describe them to anyone as very attractive and vivacious women. She never thought herself attractive—cute maybe, but not attractive. Lou was the rugged tomboy of the group who only wore ripped jeans and T-shirts growing up. She had curly auburn hair and hazel eyes with an hourglass figure she didn't like showing.

Marianne would describe Lou as a loyal friend who was brutally honest, attractive, and someone who always fought for the underdog. In her words, a "real bad ass." This is her story, which just so happens to be shared.

SINCERELY,

Chapter 1

THE CLIENT

One day Lou was at her private investigation office when a woman named Sarah Coral entered. She was a woman in her early forties, very attractive and well dressed. Sarah had long blond hair and wore a very large diamond on her ring finger.

Lou walked over to Sarah and introduced herself. "I'm Lou, how can I help you?"

Sarah replied, "Hello Lou, my name is Sarah Coral. I got your name from a friend of mine who said you can help me."

Lou smiled and asked, "What would you like me to do for you?"

Before Sarah answered her question she asked, "Lou, that's a strange name for a woman, is that short for something?"

Lou continued to smile and replied, "Yes."

Sincerely,

Sarah just smiled back. "Your office is not what I expected It is decorated quite tastefully. I love your antique oak desk; it goes well with your leather chairs. The rosary hanging behind your desk is a little interesting."

Lou once again smiled said, "I'm glad you like my office, can I ask what brings you here? I'm sure it was not to check out my office."

Sarah's eyes began to tear up. "I have been married to my husband, Jack Coral, for twenty years... we were high school sweethearts. We built an amazing life together. My husband owns Coral Construction."

"Yes, I have seen your husband's business signs all over town." Lou responded.

Sarah began to cry, "I think my husband is cheating on me. I just need proof whether he is or not."

Lou asked Sarah, "What makes you think your husband is cheating on you?"

As Lou handed Sarah a tissue, she answered "He's staying out later than usual and he's been going away on supposed business trips."

Listening to Sarah's concerns, Lou asked, "Do you have any other reason why? Have you seen him with anyone else? I mean, I'm sure you have your concerns and I'm not going to argue them. I just need a little more information."

Sarah becoming disconcerted by Lou's questions. "What other information do you need? I am telling you my husband is cheating, shouldn't that be good enough?"

2

Trying to reassure Sarah that she is on her side, Lou said, "Listen, working late and going away more is not much for me to go on. What about phone calls? Is he getting text messages and phone calls late at night? When he gets a text message does he leave the room so you don't see it? Not to pry, are you and your husband still intimate with one another?"

Sarah becoming uncomfortable with the questioning and became defensive "Yes, my husband does leave the room when he gets a text message. That is something he never did before. As for the phone calls, yes, on more than one occasion he has gotten phone calls late at night that were not work-related. As for my sex life, I would rather keep that information to myself. Now, will you take my case?

Lou took a deep breath and agreed to take her case, "Please give any information you may have on Jack. Where he hangs out? What job sites is he working at? Do you have a picture of Jack?

Sarah reached into her pocketbook and handed her a picture of Jack. As Sarah was heading towards the door she turned to Lou," I believe he will be at the Keystone Bar tonight; it seems to be his new hang out.

Before walking out the door she turned to Lou one more time, "You must look at me like I'm a joke, some stuck up rich woman coming in to hunt down her husband to see if he's cheating."

Lou stood by her desk with no facial expression, "No, what I see is a woman who has depended on her husband to survive in this world instead of making her way in this world. I will be sorry for you if he is

Sincerely,

cheating. I am sure you will do what most of my other clients do – take your husband to the cleaners."

Sarah, furious with Lou's response, said "How can you do this for a living? You are the most unprofessional person I have ever come across. I truly hope you are as good as they say you are."

Lou just smiled. "I am, please leave me your contact information and I will let you know what I find out.

As she pulled up to the Keystone she had an unsettling feeling, but brushed it off as just nerves. When she walked into the Keystone she headed right to the bar. From its location she could see who was coming and going. Coolly taking a seat, she placed her pocketbook on the bar. Her pocketbook had a small recorder sewn into its liner.

The Keystone was a small and simple dive bar with a couple of pool tables and a juke box. The tables had small candles on them. The bar had a lot of Keystone Cop silent movie posters from 1912-1917. The owner's name was Joe and his great grandfather apparently was a big fan of the movies. While Lou was waiting to see if Jack showed up, she began to talk to Joe about all the movie posters on the wall. When she looked up, she noticed Jack had arrived with a woman.

The woman was five foot six, slim build, brown hair; she looked to be in her early twenties. She was very well dressed, wearing her expensive designer jeans and white button down shirt with a pair of brown leather cowboy boots. Jack was a very good looking man in his forties; his hair was salt and pepper, he had a nice build to him. He was wearing a white T-shirt and jeans. The two sat a table and ordered a couple of beers. Lou watched as they talked and laughed together until a slow song came on the jukebox. Jack and the unknown woman began to slow dance. When the song finished the two returned to the table. Shortly after, the two made their way out of the bar. Lou waited a few minutes before exiting after them.

When Lou walked out to the parking lot she saw Jack and the unknown woman embrace in a kiss. Lou took the picture she needed and began to walk to her car. As she did, she could hear someone walking behind. It was Jack.

Jack began to yell to Lou, "Excuse me, I know you can fucking hear me."

Lou turned around and said, "Can I help you?"

Jack with anger in his voice replied, "I know who the fuck you are, you're that detective bitch who goes around catching cheating spouses. I saw your article. Listen, I will give you ten thousand for any video or pictures you've got."

Lou turned to Jack and said, "I have no idea what you're talking about. I was sitting here waiting for a date that never showed up."

Jack's voice began to rise. "Listen you dumb fucking bitch, I know you took pictures of me with that woman! Now give me your camera and we can call it a night."

Lou looked at Jack and replied, "Listen, I still have no idea what you're talking about. Why are you getting so angry? I was the one who was stood up! I should be the one who's angry!" Lou, with a grin on her face, went back to walking to her car. All at once she could hear footsteps running towards her, but before she could turn around Jack grabbed her by the back of her head and slammed it on the hood of a car. Lou became dizzy and before she knew it, Jack had dragged her behind the dumpster located in the parking lot of the Keystone.

When Lou could comprehend what was going on Jack once again asked her for the photo she took. Lou again denied taking pictures of Jack and the unknown woman.

Jack, rage in his eyes, began to yell, "YOU DUMB BITCH GIVE ME THE FUCKING PICTURES!"

Lou yelled back, "I DON'T KNOW WHAT THE FUCK YOU ARE TALKING ABOUT! NOW GET THE FUCK AWAY FROM ME!"

Jack forcefully grabbed Lou by the head and smashed it into the dumpster, cracking the back of her skull. Lou dropped to the ground and Jack proceeded to kick her in her rib cage.

While lying on the ground Lou began to think of her father and how he taught her to box at a very young age. She could hear him saying, "Kid, hands up, always protect your face." She flashed back to watching her father shaving; he always shaved with a navy blue cup filled with shaving cream and his shaving brush.

Just then she felt extreme sharp pain on her face. Jack stomped on her face with the heel of his boot, breaking her nose. While lying on the ground, drifting in and out of consciousness she could hear her father's voice saying, "Kid, if you ever feel you have no way out of situation with an assailant, kick the fucker in the balls! He will drop to his knees and this will give you enough time to get away."

As she lay on the ground she began to pray to God to give her strength to stand up. As she was praying she could feel herself begin to stand, she could feel her legs and arms shaking as she pulled herself up from the ground with every bit of strength she could muster. Jack looked shocked to see the woman he just beat suddenly standing before him. He could see the blood running down her face and he could tell she was fighting to stand.

She stood looking at Jack with no fear in her eyes. She knew she only had one chance to get away before he would kill her. She could tell by Jack's eyes that he was getting ready to attack again. Jack began to come towards her. With all her might, Lou kicked Jack in the balls, dropping him to his knees.

With her legs still shaking, she ran towards her car, grabbing her pocketbook off the ground. Swiftly, she took out her key to unlock the door. She could hear Jack screaming in the background. "YOU FUCKING BITCH! I WILL FUCKING KILL YOU! DO HEAR ME?! I WILL FUCKING KILL YOU!"

Lou sat in her car, hands shaking, and she began to cry. Just as she was going to pull out of the parking lot of the Keystone she saw Jack come out

Sincerely,

from behind the dumpster. As she drove by him he yelled, "FUCK YOU!"

While Lou was driving, she could feel herself begin to pass out. She pulled over to the side of the road and called 911. She told the operator she had just been attacked by Jack Coral at the Keystone. She explained she was bleeding and felt like she was going to pass out. The operator tried to keep Lou talking as long as she could until help arrived.

When Lou awoke she was in the hospital and everything appeared blurry at first, but as her eyes adjusted to her surroundings she could see the doctor standing by her bed. The doctor looked at her curiously and said, "You are very lucky to be alive, sustaining these injuries." Lou tried to sit up in the bed and felt a sharp pain in her side. Her head was throbbing and she began to run her hand across the back. Her head had been shaved and she could feel staples in her scalp. She began to cry as the doctor explained he had to give her stitches across the bridge of her nose from where Jack had broken it. She had four broken ribs and his main concern was her fractured skull. There were twenty-six staples in the back of her head and according to her MRI she had some swelling in the brain.

As her head was spinning from all the information the doctor had given her, she heard a familiar and comforting voice. "Hey kid, how are you?" It was her father Michael, and as soon as she saw him she began to cry even harder. Michael hugged his daughter gently, with hidden rage in his heart for the man who did this to her. With tears in his eyes he finally said, "It's okay, you're safe now."

Remembering it was the memory of his words that saved her, she looked up at her father and said, "You know Pop…it's because of you I am alive."

At that he smiled softly and said, "I love you kid." He then looked at Lou and with a stern voice said, "I think it's time you come home. Jack's in jail and you're going to need your family to help you get through this. I do not want to hear any excuses why you cannot move back home. I can't handle another phone call like the one I received, so you are coming back to Rhode Island."

Trying to show her father she was not afraid to stay in Texas she responded, "What about my business Pop? I made a life here, I can't let some scumbag piece of shit ruin that for me! I won't!"

Michael could feel his voice start to rise. "What business?! YOUR COVER IS BLOWN! YOUR PICTURE AND THE NAME OF YOUR BUSINESS ARE ALL OVER THE FUCKING NEWS! YOU'RE COMING HOME AND THAT'S IT!"

To break the tension he looked at his daughter and began to chuckle. "Maybe you'll become a professional nose model."

Lou began to laugh, holding her ribs, and said, "You're an asshole."

Just then Lou's mother Nancy entered the room and as soon as she saw her daughter she began to cry. "What did that man do to you?" she began, then looked

Sincerely,

at Michael and said, "This is your fault; she has always wanted to be like you and look where that got her."

Lou, upset with her mother, began to defend her father. "Mom stop, it's not Pop's fault. I chose this career."

Michael just sat quietly, he knew in his heart Nancy was right. He knew he should have tried harder to change his daughter's mind.

Lou's stepfather entered the room saying, "I knew I had the right room, I could hear your the arguing as I came down the hall." Ronnie walked over to Lou's bed, gave her a kiss on her forehead and asked, "How are you doing? What are the doctors saying?"

Before she could answer her mother started crying. She tried to comfort her. "Mom I'm okay, really!"

Nancy cried out, "Look what that man did to your face, you could have died!"

Michael looked over at his ex-wife and said, "Nancy, she is going to be fine, she's going to be moving back to Rhode Island."

Lou was just about to respond to her father's comment when she saw her brother enter her hospital room. He began, "Lou, don't you think this is a little dramatic to get me to come to Texas?" She smiled upon seeing him. He walked over to her and gave her a big hug. "I spoke with the doctors, they are going to keep you here for a few days for observation. I gave them my number if anything comes up during the night." Lou felt comforted, knowing her brother was with her.

Michael looked over at Lou. "Could I have the keys to your office?"

"Why?"

"I just want to go check things out. Do you have a problem with me going to your office?"

"No, my keys are in my pocketbook." Lou grinned at her father and said, "Always a cop." Michael just winked at her.

After a few hours of visiting in the hospital they could see Lou was getting tired and wanted to sleep. Nancy told her that they were going to stay at her house until she was released from the hospital. Later that evening both of Lou's parents, Ronnie, and her other brother Shane arrived at her home. Knowing his sister so well, Shane asked his mother to make a list of things she wanted at the market and suggested takeout for themselves.

Nancy opened the fridge and saw just a head of lettuce, carrots, a tomato, cheese, and milk. Nancy began to laugh and said, "You called it, she is the only girl I know who lives in the state that loves steak, but prefers being a vegetarian!"

Ronnie was watching Michael walk through the house and headed over to him. "What are you looking for?"

"I don't really know. The only thing I know is that bastard should never get out of jail. If he does I will be the first and last person he ever sees."

"Yeah, stand in line… do you want me to go with you to Lou's office tomorrow?"

11

Sincerely,

Michael shook his head no. "I'd rather have you at the hospital keeping Nancy from going crazy. I know she blames me for what happened and maybe she's right, but you and I both know Lou is very thick-headed and she usually does what she wants."

Ronnie tried reassure Michael that he shouldn't feel guilty for what happened to Lou, and told him not to pay any mind to Nancy, she didn't mean it. With a smile on his face Ronnie looked over to him and said, "Michael, do you remember when we tried to teach Lou how to ride a bike? Do remember how many times she fell on the ground and each time she fell that girl just kept getting up? She wasn't going to stop till she rode that bike without training wheels! Lou has always been the girl that no matter how many times she has fallen down in life, she always lands right back on her feet."

Michael's eyes began to fill up. "I know you're right, but this guy almost broke her. I want her back in Rhode Island to keep her safe."

Ronnie agreed; it was time to get her back home.

The next morning Michael got up early to head to Lou's office. On the way he stopped to grab a news-paper and a coffee. The front page of the newspaper read in big letters:

MILLIONAIRE ARRESTED FOR ATTEMPTED MURDER OF LOCAL PRIVATE INVESTIGATOR

Michael just stared at the picture of the man who tried to kill his child. As he sat staring he said to himself, "Jack, you just fucked with the wrong family."

When Michael arrived at Lou's office he noticed that the door was unlocked. He drew his gun and walked inside. He noticed her file cabinets had been opened, and files were scattered all over the floor. He cautiously began to walk down the hall where Lou kept her copy machine.

When he turned on the light he saw spray painted on the wall:

YOU SHOULD OF DIED

Michael punched the wall and began to yell, "MAYBE YOU SHOULD DIE!! WHEN I FIND YOU I WILL FUCKING KILL YOU!!"

Michael realized there was more to this case than just the tracking of a married man. He contacted the police and waited for them to arrive. When the police arrived they asked Michael if anything was missing. "How the hell am I supposed to know?! Do you think Jack Coral had anything to do with this?"

The police officer answered, "No, your daughter was working for us, we hired her to work on some cold cases."

Michael suddenly looked confused. "What do you mean cold cases? She told me she followed cheating spouses."

Sincerely,

The officer chuckled and said, "Then you really don't know your daughter. She has helped us solve two major cold cases."

Michael with a look of anger on his face replied, "I guess not." The police officer informed Michael that Lou was working on a case of a possible serial killer but her lead went cold. Michael was so upset with what the officer was telling him that he walked out of Lou's office and went to his car. He thought to himself, *She lied to me. My daughter lied to me all these years, she lied.*

He was so angry at Lou he drove straight to the hospital to confront her. When he entered her room ready to scream at her, he saw his daughter sleeping in the bed with a stuffed animal her brother had purchased for her at the hospital gift shop. At that moment Michael didn't see his adult daughter who lied; he saw the little girl he raised and always swore to protect.

He sat down next to Nancy, who asked, "Did you find anything at her office?"

"No." He just sat and stared at his daughter with a smile on his face and thought, *She is just like me. Maybe Nancy was right, maybe I should have talked her out of this career.*

A week passed and Lou was released from the hospital. When she arrived at her home her mother Nancy was waiting for her. Michael and Ronnie helped Lou into the house and carried in her bags. Lou wanted to prove to her family that she was fine and was okay to be left alone. Inside she wanted to scream. *Please don't leave!! I'm afraid.* As bad as she wanted to, she knew in her heart she had to face her fear and stay alone in Texas until she sold her house.

Nancy looked at Lou with tears in her eyes and said, "I don't think it's a good idea that we leave. It's your first night back in the house."

Lou looked at her mother, trying not to cry, and said, "It's okay Mom, really, I am fine. I just want to get back into a normal routine. Besides, you have been gone from home for a week and you need to get back to your life too. I'm sorry about all this. Once my house sells, I will be moving back home, don't worry."

Listening to the conversation, Michael could to tell by Lou's face that she really didn't want them to leave, but he knew his daughter had to prove to herself that she was okay to be alone. Nancy hugged her daughter and told her she would call her when she landed. Ronnie let Lou know if she needed them to stay longer they would.

Michael hugged his daughter, smiled and said, "If you need me ….you better call me."

Lou hugged her father. "I will, I promise."

After everyone left the first thing Lou wanted to do was to finally take a good shower back in her own place. She grabbed herself a pair of grey sweatpants and a white T-shirt and headed to the bathroom. As she began to get undressed she looked in the mirror for the first time since her assault. When she took her shirt off she could see how black and blue her rib cage was.

As she stood staring at the mirror she did not see herself, she saw a woman who had been badly

Sincerely,

beaten, not only physically but mentally. She grabbed a hand mirror from her vanity, angling it so she could see the reflection of the back of her head. She no longer had her curly hair, it was now shaved. She began to run her fingers across the staples in her scalp. She became so enraged by the sight of herself that she threw her hand mirror at the wall. The glass shattered and Lou collapsed to the floor and began to cry. It took everything she had to pull herself together.

Later on that night she made herself something to eat. After she finished her dinner she put her dishes in the dishwasher, walked into the living room, and sat on the couch to watch TV. While flipping through the channels a news clip of Jack Coral being brought into the courthouse appeared on the television. The news reporter stated that he had been denied bail.

Lou stood up and began to scream at the TV, "I LIVED! DO YOU HEAR ME?! YOU DIDN'T KILL ME YOU PIECE OF SHIT, I LIVED!"

Just then Lou was surprised to hear a knock at the door. Wary since she was not expecting anyone, she grabbed the knife she kept duct taped under her dining room table for added protection and walked towards the door. When she peeked out of the window she was relieved to see a familiar face. With a big smile on her face she opened the door to see her best friend Marianne. She was so happy to see her she began to cry and asked, "What are you doing here?"

Marianne hugged Lou and replied, "Did you think I wouldn't show up? You were with me when I had the pins in my hip at the age of twelve. Of course I am coming here to see you!" After pausing for a moment and looking hard at Lou, she said lovingly, "You look like shit, by the way."

The two hugged and began to laugh. Marianne wanted to cry when she saw what Jack did to her best friend; it took everything she had to hold back the tears. Marianne went out to her car to grab her luggage, some pizza, and the bottle of wine she had picked up on the way to Lou's house.

Lou smiled apologetically. "I just ate supper."

"The pizza is for after we get drunk." The two of them began to laugh.

Lou looked at Marianne and asked, "How long are you here for?"

"I am only here for a couple of days and if you need me longer then I am here longer." Marianne then laughed. "That's the perks of owning your business."

Lou was overjoyed and comforted that her friend was going to stay with her. She wanted to tell Marianne that she was afraid to be alone in the house. She wanted to tell her that Jack broke her. Instead, she just hugged her friend and said, "Thank you for being here."

Marianne opened the bottle of wine and said, "Let's get drunk." The two sat on the couch laughing about all the crazy things they did in their younger days. Marianne was right; after the wine was gone they were happy to have the pizza.

The next morning when Lou and Marianne got up, Marianne suggested they get out of the house and go for breakfast. Lou was hesitant about leaving the house due to her appearance. Marianne, with a look of admiration, told her, "Seriously Lou, how many black eyes did you get when we were kids? You were constantly getting into fights and we still went out, shiner and all! You need to get back to the girl who didn't give a shit about what other people thought!"

Lou sat for a moment lost in thought, almost as if she were just remembering who she was. She looked at Marianne with a smile and said, "You're right, if I stay home he wins."

The two arrived at a diner called Breakfast Starts Here. It was a small diner with 1950's décor. The tables had red and white chairs with chrome legs and white tabletops. The pictures on the wall were photos of famous actors, actresses, and singers from the 50s. The jukebox was playing 50's music.

When they entered the diner you could hear a pin drop; everyone just stopped and looked at Lou and Marianne. Marianne became so upset at everyone staring at them that she began to shout. "WHAT IS MY FLY DOWN?! IS THAT WHY EVERYONE IS STARING?!"

Lou chuckled and said, "Yes, your fly is down."

Marianne looked at Lou in disbelief and said, "Really?" Lou grinned and said yes. Marianne, with her face red from embarrassment, looked at everyone in the diner and said, "Thanks for letting me know!"

The waitress walked the two ladies to their table, located in the back of the diner. She looked at Lou and said, "I thought you might want some privacy away from the onlookers." With sympathy in her eyes she handed Lou her menu and coffee and finished, "I think you're one of the bravest women I know…not many people go up against Jack Coral. I'm sorry about what happened to you. I will be back in few minutes to take your order."

Marianne not knowing what to say to her friend, whose eyes were beginning to tear up, began to mimic the waitress. "'You're one of the bravest people I know'—no I am one of the bravest people she knows, I walked in here with my fly down. Thank God I was wearing underwear…I look like I could be in 70's porn!"

Lou began to laugh so hard she spit her coffee out of her mouth. Marianne laughing and talking at the same time said, "What? I didn't have time to wax! I was in a rush to come see you."

The waitress returned to the table to take their order. Lou ordered a veggie omelet and Marianne ordered two eggs over easy with bacon. While waiting for their food to come Marianne asked Lou if her parents knew what she really did for a living. Lou looked Marianne in the eye and said, "No, only you, Bella, and Joanne know. I don't like the fact that you three know what I do. My work is obviously dangerous. I don't ever want to drag any of you into my work."

Marianne laughed and replied, "That's never going to happen."

With a smile on Lou's face she replied, "I know."

Sincerely,

Marianne in a high pitched voice said, "OH MY GOD, guess who I ran into in Pawtucket?!" Lou, with a confused look on her face, asked who. Marianne replied, "Father Joe, he is running a homeless shelter now. He asked how you were doing. I'm not going to lie to a priest so I told him what you were really up to. He told me to tell you that he will keep you in his prayers and if you ever want to talk he's always free to go for coffee."

Lou began to feel a sense of security as soon as Marianne mentioned Father Joe. She then asked Marianne how he was doing. Marianne told Lou that he was doing great, but that his appearance had changed a bit. He dressed more in street clothes than in a cassock. Lou was surprised to hear that; she always remembered Father Joe teaching CCD classes and getting everyone ready to make their confirmation.

When she was getting into a lot of fights in school and getting in trouble at home, the one person she always talked to was Father Joe. He would always ask why she felt a need to get into so many fights. Lou's response was always, "I don't like people who pick on other people for being different." Father Joe knew what she meant. He would always remind her to try to walk away and not to fight. Lou's famous response to him was, "I'll try, I can't promise...but I can try."

Marianne told Lou once she moved back to Rhode Island she should look him up. She thought it would be a good idea for her to talk to someone about everything that had just happened to her.

After they finished their breakfast they got into Lou's car and decided to go thrifting at a few local secondhand stores. While driving, Marianne asked Lou if she missed having a normal life.

"Yes," Lou responded, and explained how she never wanted to drag another person into the life she chose.

Marianne with a big smile said, "Please tell me you at least have sex?"

Lou began to laugh. "Yes, I have sex. I actually had very good sex."

Marianne let out a sigh of relief. "Thank God, now details please."

Lou laughed. "A lady never tells, but I will tell you handcuffs come in handy." When Marianne laughed and asked if she could borrow them sometime, Lou answered, "I'll give you one of my sets."

Marianne stopped laughing and looked at Lou. "Sets... plural...you have sets. You are a kinky cowgirl!"

When they arrived at the first thrift shop, Marianne's face lit up like a Christmas tree. She could not get over all the unique items they had in the store.

While walking down an aisle grabbing cowboy boots and vintage leather jackets, she saw a woman approach Lou. Marianne walked over to where Lou was standing. The woman in front of Lou was Jack Coral's wife. Lou introduced Sarah to Marianne. Sarah looked at Lou's bruised face and began to apologize for what her husband had done. Lou just stood and

Sincerely,

stared at Sarah with a rage in heart that she never felt before, nor did she understand why.

Sarah began to tell Lou that Jack asked her to stand by him during the trial. She told Lou that she was going to divorce him and move out of Texas to another state. She explained that she needed to start a new life for her and her children. Lou just kept on staring at Sarah, not really knowing how to respond to what she was saying. The only thing she could think of was that if it wasn't for her asking her to follow Jack, she would not be standing there having this conversation with her face looking like it was hit by a bus.

As Sarah walked out of the store, Marianne just looked at Lou and asked, "Are you alright? You didn't say anything; you just stood there not saying a word."

Lou wanted to tell Marianne about the rage she felt in her heart towards Sarah but instead just said, "She's really not worth giving her my opinion about her husband. I really don't care what happens to her."

Marianne paused. She knew Lou was holding back something but said, "Okay...let's shop then."

When they arrived back at Lou's house the two grabbed a couple of beers and sat on the deck. Lou asked Marianne if she would go with her to her office so she could pack it up and get ready for her move back to Rhode Island. Marianne obliged. "Sure, do I get to read some of your case files?"

Lou laughed. "No...well...maybe a few."

Marianne exclaimed, "Yes!!" with loveable childlike excitement.

The next morning the two grabbed a couple of coffees and muffins and headed to Lou's office. When Lou opened the door to her office it was spotless and had the smell of fresh paint.

Lou looked at Marianne and said, "Wow, it took me going into the hospital to get my landlord to finally paint my office space and the cleaning lady to clean it!" Her father and Ronnie had gone to her office and cleaned and painted so she would never know what was sprayed on her wall.

As Lou was packing up her files, she asked Marianne to help her lift the carpet. Marianne looked surprised but agreed to help her. Under the rug Lou had cut out a section of the floor. She began to hand Marianne file folders. Then she pulled out cash and a couple of knives. Marianne just stood there not knowing what to say.

Lou looked at Marianne and said, "Did you really think I would leave my cold case files where everyone can get their hands on them?"

Marianne just looked at Lou with amazement. "I never realized how involved you are with your work. Why did you hide so much cash?"

"This is my get-out-of-town-quick money."

Still not knowing what to say, Marianne managed, "Oh yeah…everyone should have that." Curious about what her friend did for a living, she asked, "How many cold cases have you worked on? How many did you help solve?"

Lou, rather uncomfortable about discussing her work, answered, "I solved four cold cases and the one I was working on was for a serial killer they call Sincerely. This lunatic severs his victims' heads and removes their teeth. At every murder site he leaves a note, Sincerely. The police have been on this case for years."

Marianne, with concern in her eyes for her friend, asked, "Why would you want to chase someone like that? Have you thought about a career change? How close did you get to him?"

Lou just laughed. "I am good at what I do, I love what I do. I think I was getting close to him, I could feel it! The fucked up thing about him is he leaves the victims' heads in such random places, like a swing in a playground or on a bike path."

Marianne sat listening to her friend discussing this as if it was nothing. The only thing she could say was, "What a sick fuck."

Lou nodded. "Yes, the funny part is the note he leaves is always on a white piece of paper with the word Sincerely. It's typed on an old-school typewriter."

As Marianne sat at Lou's desk chair listening to her friend talk about the serial killer Sincerely, the only thing she could think was this was not a career choice, this was a death wish.

The next day Marianne was getting ready to go back home to Rhode Island. She hugged her friend and said, "I will see you when you come back home."

Lou thanked Marianne for coming to Texas. She told her that she did not think she could get through one of the most difficult times of her life without her. As Marianne was boarding the plane, Lou shouted, "SEE YOU IN A COUPLE OF MONTHS, AND YOU BETTER HAVE A BEER WAITING FOR ME!"

Chapter 2

THE MOVE

A few months passed and Lou was able to sell her house. She received a good price on the home she once loved. Her house was a small Cape with a lot of charm. It had two bedrooms, a living room with a fireplace, and a large kitchen with an island. It was cozy and people always told her that when they walked into her house it always felt like home.

The day before her move back to Rhode Island, she sat on her deck for one last time. She sat drinking coffee out of her favorite coffee mug, took a deep breath and said to herself, "Okay, you can do this."

As she was sipping she began to reflect on what happened that night with Jack Coral. She began to run her fingers through her hair; she could feel the scar on the back of her head. She ended up with a scar over the bridge of her nose too. The doctors did a good job at leaving minimal scarring. She was grateful at least for that.

The next day the moving truck showed up to bring her belongings back to Rhode Island. Lou took a plane home and when she arrived she was greeted by her mother Nancy. Nancy gave her daughter an immense hug and said, "God, I am so happy you are finally home."

When Lou walked out of the airport, she looked at her mother and said, "Oh my god, you can tell fall is coming, the air has that crisp fall smell!"

Nancy laughed. "It's been a long time since you've been to New England to enjoy your favorite season."

Lou smiled. "I really do love the fall, Mom. I'm looking forward to all the fall activities that go on here; it's good to be back home."

When Lou arrived at her mother's house she was greeted by her siblings, her stepfather Ronnie, and her friends Bella and Marianne. Nancy made a great Italian dinner that consisted of meatballs and spaghetti, a tomato and mozzarella cheese platter, veggie lasagna, homemade Italian bread, and a beautiful salad. After dinner Lou and her two friends sat around her mother's in ground pool. Bella asked Lou how she was doing.

Lou replied, "I'm better now that I am home. I was thinking… maybe it's time for a career change."

Sincerely,

Marianne, overly happy to hear these words asked, "What are you going to do? You have been doing investigation for most of your adult life."

Lou looked at the two of them and said, "I want a life, I want a job that's not going to kill me. It's time for me to live my life."

Marianne replied to that statement by saying, "Then let's start enjoying our lives, let's go out for a few drinks!"

Lou and Bella stood up and said, "Let's go!"

The three ladies jumped into Bella's car and headed towards the first bar they could find. The three ladies walked into the bar and ordered their first round of beers. They began to talk about their childhood experiences.

Marianne looked over at Lou with a big grin on her face and asked, "Do you remember when we were at Newport Creamery? We had just ordered a couple of brownie sundaes and we had been dating our boyfriends for a while, and I asked you if you had sex yet? You looked at me and said 'Did you?,' Then we both looked at each other and admitted we had!" The two ladies started laughing and couldn't believe that they lost their virginity at the same time.

Bella chimed in and said, "I remember the two of you dated them for a few years."

As the beers were flowing Bella blurted out, "Hey Lou, would you consider renting an apartment? There's one for rent next to my house. This way you don't have to live at your parents' house and it will give you time to figure out where you want to live."

L.A. Brien

Lou thought about it. "Bella, that's not a bad idea. I love my parents but I love my privacy too! Let's go look at it tomorrow." After a great night of much catching up, they finished their drinks and headed home.

The next morning Bella picked Lou up at her parents' house to look at the apartment she mentioned the night before. The apartment was located off Newport Avenue in Pawtucket. The landlord greeted Lou and Bella at the apartment. Bella was acquainted with the landlord and she thanked him for letting Lou see the place on such short notice. When Lou walked in the first thing she noticed was the French doors that divided the living room and dining room. The kitchen was an eat-in with a lot of cupboard space. It had one bedroom. Lou fell in love with the place immediately. She even loved the fact her father Michael only lived a block away and Bella lived right down the street. Lou felt it was a godsend and a safe place to live. She also couldn't believe how affordable the rent was; she was able to write a check out paying for six months of rent.

A week later Lou was settling into her new apartment. She gave it the same cozy feeling that her home in Texas had. She had her white couches with throw pillows on them, her dining room had a pub style table in the corner, and she had a hand carved trunk with an antique typewriter on it. Next to the typewriter was a picture of her father. She kept the picture facing a doorway. She felt safe knowing that was the first thing she saw when she walked into her home. Her bedroom was her favorite room in the house. She deco-

29

rated using all earth tones. The last item she hung up in her room was her crucifix. Lou always said her prayers at night since she was a child, standing in front of her crucifix.

After she finished unpacking her decorations she opened a box marked "PRIVATE" which contained all of her knives, mace, and an aerosol hairspray can with a lighter. She duct taped a knife under the dining room table, placed one knife under the coffee table, and the hairspray and lighter in the bathroom. The mace she kept on her nightstand and another knife was placed between her mattress and box spring. When she was finished placing her weapons around the house she stood in front of the crucifix and thanked God for her new apartment and for surviving the night Jack attacked her.

After she said her prayers, she poured herself a cup of coffee and grabbed her laptop to start her job hunting. As she was looking for jobs online she started laughing, thinking to herself how one finds a job when all you have ever done is private investigations. "I can see my résumé," she said out loud, and started to giggle. She thought her tagline would be "Hire me or I will find out all your dirty little secrets."

As she was sipping her coffee she noticed a bartending job at the Italian Club. She thought that would be a great place to apply since most of her family frequented that particular club. The next day she went to the Italian Club to apply for the job. She met with the head bartender, whose name was Brian. Brian had her fill out an application and explained to her how the bar got busy especially during football season. He told her that she would work solo; she would be responsible for serving drinks and taking food orders.

She felt confident that she would be able to handle the job and to her surprise Brian asked her if she could start that coming Saturday. She graciously accepted and thanked him for the opportunity. When she got into her car she called Marianne and Bella to see if they would like to grab dinner and celebrate her finding a new job so quickly.

The girls met up for dinner and started ordering appetizers and drinks. Marianne asked Lou if she was ready to get back to work. She was concerned that it was too soon after her attack. Lou understood Marianne's concern; she had the same concerns herself. She looked at her friend with a false confidence in her eyes and said, "Yes, I'm ready! I need to get back to a normal life. I can't let what that bastard did to me affect my life any longer, I won't."

Hearing this Marianne smiled and said, "You are one of the strongest people I know."

Lou laughed. "No not really, I just can't let one tragedy rule my life." What she really wanted to say but could not admit even to herself was that she felt defeated, and afraid. She would not admit that to her friends or her family.

Bella looked at her friends and said, "Enough of all this talk, we should be concentrating on finding Lou a man! So...anyone in here look good to you?"

Lou just started laughing as she looked around the room and replied, "NO."

Sincerely,

Bella, not giving up on the topic said, "What if you let me set you up on a blind date?"

At that point Marianne chimed in. "Really? Who do you know who is single? Who do you think would be good enough for our friend?"

Bella, feeling confident on finding Lou a date said, "I know people, and besides my husband has friends who are single. Maybe she could just use someone to have fun with, and pass the time; you never know what might come of it."

At this Marianne started laughing. "I love your husband and all but I have met some of his friends and the answer is no."

Lou just sat in amazement as she watched her two best friends trying to find her a Mister Right.

Bella looked over at her again. "Lou, please tell Marianne I am more than capable of finding you a man."

Lou just laughed and said, "If you can find someone that Marianne would approve of then I will go on a date."

Bella responded, "Well, I guess you're going to remain single. We both know she will never approve of anyone!" At that point Lou asked for the check and wanted to call it a night.

Saturday came and she was excited about starting her new job. She got up and made herself a cup of coffee. She walked back into her bedroom and opened her closet to pick out an outfit for her first day of work. After ten minutes of just staring into her closet she grabbed a pair of jeans and a white peasant top. She showered, put her makeup on, and put her hair up in a ponytail. When she arrived at work she saw a familiar face. She smiled and walked over to her father and kissed him on the cheek.

"What are you doing here?"

"It's Saturday, where else would I be?! Rumor had it that a new bartender was starting today."

Shortly after she arrived the bar began to fill up; she got a hang of pouring drinks and serving food pretty fast. At the end of her shift Brian approached her and congratulated her for doing a good job. He offered her a Friday and Sunday shift. Once again she thanked him for the opportunity.

Her father was still sitting at the bar so she sat down next to him and he bought her a drink. Michael looked over at Lou and asked, "How did you do to-night?"

She looked at her father. "Really Pop?" She started to giggle. "Not bad to be honest."

He smiled. "Good."

When Lou arrived home from her day at work she ordered herself a veggie burger and picked out a bottle of wine. She threw on grey sweatpants and a white T-shirt, poured herself a glass, and grabbed her laptop to check her emails. While scrolling through her emails she noticed one from the attorney general's office in Texas. It read:

Dear Lou,
The attorney general's office would like to in-form you the trial regarding case number 2654 The

Sincerely,

State of Texas vs Jack Coral has been scheduled. The hearing date is for January 21, 2020. We will have one of our attorneys contact you when the court date gets closer. We would like to inform you that the defendant has pled not guilty due to temporary insanity. If you have any questions please contact our office.
Sincerely yours,

> *Jaxon Milton*
> *Attorney General*

Lou sat and stared at the email for about ten minutes in disbelief that this monster was claiming an insanity plea. In a rage she grabbed the phone and called her father. "Pop, this is bullshit. I just received a letter from the attorney general's office stating that Jack put in an insanity plea. How the hell can he do this? He was perfectly sane when he smashed my head into a dumpster!"

Michael gave a heavy sigh. "Lou... listen, he is going to grasp at straws to try to get out of this. You of all people should know this. We will deal with this when the date gets closer. If you dwell on this it will eat away at you and drive you crazy! Now, relax...I will see what I can find out. Love you kid."

To this she replied, "You're right Pop; you're always right. Love you too." She hung up the phone with a sense of relief, knowing that she had her father by her side.

She finished eating her dinner and brought her plate into the kitchen. She could hear a moaning sound coming from the house next door. She giggled and thought to herself, *Well at least* someone *is getting laid.* She shut the light off in the kitchen, went into her room and put the TV on. She was happy to see an old black and white horror movie on. She loved classic horror movies.

The next morning she decided to get up early and head to Slater Park for a walk on the bike path. She could not get over what a perfect morning it was. It felt like a typical fall day, with a cool breeze and leaves beginning to change. She walked five miles and the whole while thought about how great it felt to be back home and away from the nightmare in Texas. After her walk she stopped by a local coffee shop and bought a large coffee and a muffin. As she was looking at the muffin she thought to herself, *And this is why you walk five miles.*

When she arrived at home she took a shower and put on her grey sweatpants and white T-shirt. She sat down on the couch and switched the station to the local news. She grabbed her muffin and took a bite of it.

There was a sharp pain as she bit down, and she rubbed her tongue through her mouth and realized a piece of her back tooth was missing. She ran to the bathroom to inspect the rest of her mouth and noticed she had two more that were loose. She became angry and shouted, "Thank you Jack for the constant reminder of that fucking night!"

Lou grabbed her phone and called her mother to ask if she knew of a dentist that could fix what Jack did to her mouth. Nancy asked how she cracked her

Sincerely,

tooth. She did not have the heart to tell her that it was from the night she was attacked. She told her mother it must have been from eating something. In her mind, she really wasn't lying to her mother. Nancy told Lou about a new dental practice that just opened up in the town of Lincoln not too far from her, and that his name was Dr. Tamin. He received great reviews according to her friends.

When Lou hung up the phone with her mother she called Dr. Tamin's office. The receptionist booked her appointment for the upcoming Thursday at 9:00 a.m.

When Thursday arrived Lou showed up fifteen minutes early to fill out paperwork. She could not get over how nice the office was; everything was white. White couches, white walls, the entire reception area was white. While sitting in the waiting room she began to think of a story she could tell Dr. Tamin about her teeth being loose. She didn't want to go over the whole debacle with Jack Coral again.

When she was called into Dr. Tamin's examination room the first thing she noticed was how good looking he was. Dr. Tamin was in his early forties with brown wavy hair, very tall and muscular, and had hazel eyes.

Lou sat in the dentist chair and Dr. Tamin began to ask her questions. "Nice to meet you Lou. What brings you here today?"

She instantly went into a story about how she was in a car accident recently and discovered she had a cracked tooth and some of her teeth were loose.

Dr. Tamin looked into Lou's eyes, letting them linger, and said, "Okay, let me take a look." After a few minutes of poking, he rejoined with, "You cracked your number one molar, and numbers fourteen and fifteen are very loose."

Lou looked up at Dr. Tamin with her eyes beginning to tear up. "What does that mean? Can you fix it? Am I going to lose my teeth?"

He just looked down at Lou and said, "I can fix this, I will begin by removing the teeth. We let your gums heal then I will give you three caps." Lou's eyes continued to tear up. All she could think was how many more reminders did she need about that night? She asked Dr. Tamin how long the whole process would take. "The whole process will take eight weeks. I will file down three teeth."

Before Dr. Tamin could finish, Lou's teary eyes began to change from sad to angry as she told him, "I don't need the back tooth, please give me the caps for the other two teeth."

He smiled at Lou and replied, "Okay, let's do this. Now let me discuss the cost. It will cost one thousand per tooth."

Lou's jaw hit the floor. "One thousand dollars per tooth, you want two thousand for two teeth?! Are they made of gold? Holy shit I picked the wrong field."

Dr. Tamin began to laugh. "What do you do for a living?" he asked her.

She answered, "I'm just a humble bartender sir." Dr. Tamin explained to Lou that they did have a payment plan if that would help her. Lou jokingly

Sincerely,

asked, "What happens if you don't pay? Do you take the teeth back?"

Dr. Tamin just smiled and said, "Sometimes." He began to laugh. "I am really going to enjoy having you as a patient."

A week later Dr. Tamin removed Lou's back tooth and filed down her other two teeth. After the procedure he told her that he would see her in a few weeks for her caps.

Chapter 3

THE NEIGHBOR

That Saturday morning Lou returned home from her walk in Slater Park and went to the kitchen. She grabbed a bottle of water, and while standing there a moment she heard the lingering sound of loud trucks close to her apartment. She curiously peered out the window and noticed moving trucks next door. She thought to herself she had just heard moaning coming from that house, maybe it was that tenant's last night in the house and they decided to go out with a bang. She started to giggle and said out loud to herself, "Well I hope the new neighbor is nice!" and went about the rest of her day until she had to go work.

She went to get into her car and like any nosy neighbor, tried to catch a glimpse of the stranger next door. She got a peek of him standing outside on the walk barking instructions to the movers. She noticed that he was tall and wearing a baseball cap, however she was disappointed she could not see his face.

When she got home from work it was around 1:30 a.m. She was exhausted, but took a shower and put on her sweatpants and T-shirt then headed for the kitchen. She poured herself a bowl of cereal and went into the living room to watch a little TV before heading to bed. About an hour later she headed to her bedroom to call it night, and did her normal routine. She stood in front of her crucifix to say her prayers, and put the TV on low. The sound of the TV always helped her fall asleep.

As she was lying in bed she had a very unsettling feeling that someone was watching her, so she got out of bed and looked through her blinds. She saw the curtains of the house next door close as she looked out her window.

Startled, she closed the blinds and curtains and grabbed her knife from between her mattress and box spring, placing it under her pillow. Perhaps she was overreacting, but better safe than sorry.

The next day she woke up around eleven in the morning. She made herself a cup of coffee and sat at the kitchen table. She looked out her kitchen window and saw her new neighbor getting into his car. As she watched him pull out of his driveway she thought to herself that last night might have been her imagination. Just then Lou's cellphone rang.

It was Bella. "Hey chick, what are you doing later? Do you want to go shopping with me?"

"Sure why not; and where are we going shopping?"

Bella, excited that Lou said she'd like to go knowing her friend hated shopping, said, "The mall! I will pick you up in an hour."

Lou threw on a pair of jeans and a sweatshirt and waited downstairs for her friend.

When Bella arrived she rolled down her window and said, "Are you ready for a day of shopping?"

Lou giggled and said, "Yes, I am ready." While at the mall Lou told Bella what had happened the night before with her new neighbor. Bella, knowing what her friend had already been through, explained to her that maybe he'd heard a noise outside, or Lou herself pulling up early in the morning and was curious to see who it was. Lou thought to herself that Bella was probably right; he was new to the neighborhood.

After a couple hours of shopping the two sat down at the food court and ordered a couple of coffees and began to talk. Lou asked Bella how life was treating her. In true Bella fashion she responded, "My life is great, I have the most amazing husband and, knock on wood... my daughter is doing well in college."

Bella then turned the tables on to Lou. "So...tell me, how you are feeling? And do be honest, it's me you're talking to."

After a pause, Lou responded, "I am fine, I'm glad to be back home. I know you and Marianne want me to start dating, but to be honest I'm not really ready. I need to put my life back in order. Plus I really like bartending, but it's not what I want to do forever."

Sincerely,

With concern in her eyes Bella responded, "Please...tell me you are NOT thinking about going back into private investigation Lou?!"

Lou wanted to tell her yes, that was her passion. That's what made her happy. Instead she assured her friend, "No, I don't know what I want to do." At this Bella was happy.

The friends left after some time and Bella dropped Lou off back at her place. When Lou returned from the mall she put her purchases away and went into the kitchen to make a veggie burger and sweet potato fries. While Lou was cooking she could hear a woman moaning loudly. She walked over to her kitchen window and could see her new neighbor's blinds were drawn to the middle of the window. She could see his penis, and a woman who was bent and moaning.

Lou backed away from the window with her jaw dropped and quickly grabbed her cellphone to call Bella again and told her what was going on. Bella excitedly told Lou she would be at her house in literally two minutes. Literally within two minutes Lou had a knock at the door and it was Bella with a bottle of wine, smiling from ear to ear.

"Porn time!" They laughed loudly. Lou and Bella sat at the kitchen table with their glasses of wine, watching the show.

The nameless woman was shouting, "FUCK ME HARDER!"

The neighbor yelled back to the nameless woman, "YOU LIKE THAT YOU DISGUSTING BITCH!"

Bella and Lou just looked at each other and could not believe that man just yelled that to the woman. Lou started laughing. "What a freak."

The nameless woman began to shout, "FUCK ME UP THE ASS!"

Lou spit her wine all over the kitchen table and began to belly laugh, Bella joining her shortly after. The pair was in hysterics; they couldn't have stopped laughing if their lives depended on it.

That's when they heard the nameless woman yell, "Oh my God, your neighbor can see us!"

When Lou and Bella looked out the window they could see the neighbor's eyes just staring at them through the blinds. Lou and Bella dropped to the floor and sniggered like two teenage girls. Lou crawled over to her kitchen window and closed her blinds. Bella told Lou that next time she was going to bring the popcorn and thanked her for a very entertaining night.

The next morning Lou got up early to head to Slater Park for a walk. When she went out to her car she found a wine bottle on her dash with a used condom tied to it, and a note:

I hope you enjoyed the show
Here is a souvenir

Lou stood there with a look of horror on her face. She did not know what to think—her first instinct was to grab the bottle of wine and throw into a plastic bag she had in the car from the market. She got into her car and drove to Bella's house. While driving to Bel-

Sincerely,

la's house she began to think out loud. "What type of crazy person is living next to me?!"

When she arrived to Bella's she asked her to come outside. She did not want Bella's daughter to see the souvenir that her neighbor left. When Bella came outside she could see by looking at Lou that something was wrong. Lou handed Bella the note first, then the plastic bag with the bottle and condom in it. When Bella opened the bag she could not believe what she was looking at. It took a minute before she said anything. "Lou, is that a used condom?" she asked.

"Yes, Bella that is a used condom, that fucking crazy new neighbor of mine fucking left it for me. What kind of fucking crazy person does that?"

Bella told Lou that she needed to call her father and let him know what just happened. Lou wanted to call her father, but she did not want him thinking she could not take care of herself. She knew seeing what Jack did to her took a toll on him. Lou lied and told Bella that she would call her father. Bella, knowing her friend, asked, "Are you really going to call him?"

Lou replied, "Yes, I just told you I was going to." Bella then asked Lou if she wanted her to throw the bottle in the trash. Lou, not thinking before she spoke, "No, I am going to put it in my storage unit, you never know when you're going to need evidence."

Bella just stared at her friend and with a stern tone said, "What do you mean evidence? REMEMBER YOU'RE A BARTENDER, LIVE A NORMAL LIFE. You gave up your career that almost killed you! So I will ask you again, do you want me to throw the bottle out?!"

Lou, not knowing how to respond to her friend, fibbed, "Yes, I am going to throw it out. I was just kidding! I was trying to make light of the situation, I promise I am going to throw it out—and why the hell would I want to keep a used condom?! What kind of a person do you think I am?"

Bella with a smirk on her face replied, "The person I know won't throw out the bottle and knowing you, you probably have your storage unit set up like an office! Listen, I am going to trust that you are going to call your father and throw it away! For the love of God! Please…call me later."

Lou hugged her friend and promised. When she got into her car she drove right to her storage unit. She was amazed that Bella knew she probably had the unit set up like an office. When she opened her unit door she had her desk set up with pictures of Jack with newspaper clippings on the wall. She had her filing cabinets and a mini refrigerator. Wearing gloves, she put the used condom in an evidence bag and placed it in the fridge. She sat at her desk for a minute, reflecting on her conversation with Bella.

She started to think about her assault and how Jack changed her life completely. She was thinking about one thing: what Jack had said to her that night. He told her he had read an article about her. Lou knew she never did an article on her work; that would compromise everything she worked for. She grabbed everything she had on Jack and headed home. When Lou

Sincerely,

pulled up in her driveway she could see a paper on her neighbor's window. When she went upstairs to her apartment she looked out her kitchen window, and taped to her neighbor's window directly facing hers was another note:

I HOPE YOU ENJOYED YOUR PRESENT

Lou grabbed a piece of paper to respond to her neighbor's note. She wrote:

YOU'RE A SICK FUCK!!!!!

As she walked into her living room mumbling to herself about her new neighbor, she grabbed her file on Jack and began to spread everything across her coffee table. She sat and read the police report and hospital records. Her mind kept flashing back to the day she saw Sarah at the secondhand store. Lou grabbed her cellphone and called her father. "Pop, I think Jack's attack on me was a setup."

Michael with concern in his voice responded, "What do you mean?"

Lou was intent on letting her father know all the details of the night at the Keystone. "Pop, when I was leaving the Keystone, Jack said he read an article about me. What article? I never did an article."

Michael was silent for a moment; the only thing he could think of was the message that was left on Lou's office wall. He asked her what she was doing in the morning. Lou responded, "Meeting you for breakfast."

Her father laughed. "Yes, meet me at the diner in the morning around ten o'clock. Bring your files with you. I know the owner; he will give us seats in the back so we can talk."

Lou with a sense of relief answered, "Okay Pop, sounds good. Love you…see you tomorrow." After she hung up the phone she realized she had not eaten. She went into the kitchen and grabbed peppers, onions, mushrooms, broccoli, and soy sauce and placed all the ingredients in a frying pan. When she went to grab her wooden spoon she realized that she had left the note on the window. She had totally forgotten about it. As she went to remove the note she was shocked to see that her neighbor had responded to it:

YOU HAVE NO IDEA

Lou had a very uneasy feeling. She finished cooking her supper and made herself a plate then went into the living room to watch TV. While eating her dinner she was wondering what the chances were of having two encounters with two crazy people all around the same time. She thought to herself *He's probably a young guy trying to get a rise out of me.* She finished her dinner and placed her dish in the sink. She grabbed the note she wrote and turned the paper over and wrote:

HAVE A GOOD NIGHT ☺

Sincerely,

She taped the note to the window and hoped this would bring peace between and her and her new neighbor. Just then her cellphone began to ring; it was Marianne.

Marianne started to shout, "WHAT KIND OF NEIGHBOR DO YOU HAVE LIVING NEXT DOOR? HE LEFT A USED CONDOM ON YOUR CAR, WHAT THE HELL LOU?!"

Lou started laughing. "Hello to you, too. Let me guess, Bella called you?"

Marianne, still upset, began by asking, "Why was I NOT invited to the live porn show?"

Lou started laughing again and replied, "Really? I think you're more upset over that. Probably because you live in Cranston; by the time you would have gotten here the show would be over."

Marianne with sarcasm in her voice groaned, "Oh sure, use that excuse: 'you live too far away.'"

Lou giggled. "I just did. Anyways, Marianne let me call you back...my dentist's office is calling."

Lou cut her friend off and answered the other line and heard, "This is Dr. Tamin's office, we would like to schedule your appointment."

"It's already time? When does the dentist want to see me?"

"He would like to schedule your appointment for next Friday at 9:00 a.m. Is that alright?"

"I will see you then."

When she hung up the call with the dentist's office, she called Marianne back. With excitement in her voice she told Marianne that her teeth were in. She told Marianne that she was getting them next Friday. Lou hung up and went into the kitchen to make herself a cup of coffee. She took a quick glimpse out of her window again to see if her neighbor took his note down. To her surprise he left another note:

SEE YOU IN MY DREAMS

She shook her head and thought, *What a freak.* When she finished her cup of coffee she went into her bedroom to get ready for bed. She began her nightly ritual of standing in front of her crucifix to say her prayers. While she was praying she had the same unsettling feeling that she was being watched. She walked over to her window to look out of her blinds, and staring right at her through the blinds was a set of eyes.

Lou's heart began to race; she felt a sense of panic come over her. She backed away quickly and drew her curtains and began to run around the apartment to make sure all the doors were locked. She grabbed her mace and knife and placed them under her pillow. She prayed to God to keep her safe throughout the night. She had a hard time falling asleep.

The next morning Lou woke up, she thanked God for keeping her safe. She wasn't sure if she had overreacted or it was all in her head. She went to the kitchen to make herself a coffee and sat at her kitchen table. Getting ready to take a sip of her coffee, glancing toward the window, she noticed another note:

Sincerely,

I HOPE YOU HAD A GOOD NIGHT SLEEP

Lou, becoming more and more agitated by her new neighbor, grabbed a piece of paper to leave him a friendly message:

YES I DID
NOW CAN YOU PLEASE LEAVE ME ALONE!!!!!

After she taped the note up she took her shower and went to her room to get dressed. She grabbed her jeans, brown leather boots, a white tank top, and a long tan sweater. She put her makeup on and put her hair in a high ponytail. She grabbed her file on Jack and headed to the diner.

While driving she was undecided if she was going to tell her father about her new neighbor. She began to think how much he already went through with the attack. She decided not to tell him. If the situation got worse she would let him know. When she arrived her father had arranged to be seated at a table in the back of the diner so the two of them could review the files.

After they ordered breakfast Michael looked over at his daughter and asked, "Why do you think it was a setup?" Michael in the back of his mind knew it was; he remembered the message painted on her office wall.

Lou replied, "I didn't remember all the details of that night, I've been getting bits and pieces back. I think it was from the concussion. I am sure that before he attacked me he said, 'I know who you are, you're the woman in that article.'"

Michael, concerned for his daughter, asked, "Are you sure that's what he said?"

Lou became a little defensive and answered, "Yes, I am sure that's what he said. I am actually one hundred percent sure that's what he said. I am beginning to believe his wife Sarah had something to do with it."

Michael looked a little surprised by what she was saying. "Why do you think his wife was involved? What do you know about her?"

She answered her father the best she could. "I really don't know much. She came into my office and asked me to follow her husband. What I do know about her is that she is active in her community, she's been married to Jack forever and appears to be very involved with her children."

Michael and Lou finished their breakfast and Michael told Lou that he would see what he could find out about Sarah. When they were getting ready to leave the diner, Lou kissed her father on the cheek and began to giggle.

Her father gave her a curious look. "What are you giggling about?"

She looked at her father with a big smile and said, "Did you ever think that we would be working together?"

He began to laugh. "No, not in a million years."

Sincerely,

When she left the diner she went and did some much needed grocery shopping. While in the market she began to get an unsettling feeling about going home. She wasn't sure if she'd be coming home to a note on the window or some creepy set of eyes staring at her through the blinds. She began to think it would be best not to respond to any more of his notes and maybe he would just stop.

When she arrived home she put her groceries away and made herself a cup of coffee and went into the living room to check her emails. She told herself that she was not going to check the window for a note. Curiosity got the best of her. She went into the kitchen to peek through her blinds to see if the neighbor left her a note. He'd responded to her last note asking him to leave her alone and simply stated:

NO!!!!!

Lou just looked at the note and said out loud, "What the fuck?" She grabbed her cellphone and called Marianne. "Marianne you won't believe the notes my neighbor is leaving me, he's a nut job."

Marianne with confusion in her voice asked, "What do you mean notes? I thought he only left you one on your car. What is he saying?"

Lou, forgetting that she had not shared this information with her friend responded, "I think he is just pissed off because Bella and I saw him having sex, so he's been leaving notes in his window for me. I'm sure it will blow over."

Marianne, curious about the notes, began to question Lou on what they said and asked her if she'd responded. Lou was hesitant to tell her friend about the notes. Marianne, becoming impatient with Lou demanded, "I'm waiting for an answer."

Lou began to tell her about the notes, including the one she left that morning and how he responded. Marianne then asked if the note was still in the window. If it was, she wanted Lou to take a picture of it. Lou giggled at first and asked why she wanted a pic. Marianne in a sarcastic voice said, "Because I want to see it."

Lou, still giggling at her friend, agreed to take the picture. "If you keep up being so curious I'm going to give you a junior detective badge."

As Lou began to open her blind to take the picture she could see her neighbor's eyes staring at her. As Lou tried to hurry to take a pic of the note, her neighbor removed it and waved his finger back and forth motioning "no." Lou just stood staring into her neighbor's eyes and froze for one second. She could hear Marianne on the phone saying she didn't get a picture yet. Lou pointed her phone towards the window and before the neighbor could move she took a picture of him staring at her through the blinds. She immediately sent it to Marianne.

When Marianne received the picture she asked "Who the hell is that? Is that the neighbor? All I can see is eyes."

Lou with a nervous tone to her voice answered, "That's my neighbor."

Sincerely,

Marianne began to yell. "Get the fuck out of your apartment and go to Bella's! I will meet you there. Keep me on the phone until you get in your car."

Lou grabbed her keys and pocketbook and headed towards her car. When she got in she could see the silhouette of the man through the blinds. He was still watching her. As she began to back out of the driveway she could see him waving bye.

When Lou arrived at Bella's she was met outside. "Marianne already called me she is on her way," said Bella. "Lou I'm worried about you, maybe you should stay with your mother for a while or…move. I don't think you can handle the stress right now, and you shouldn't have to."

Lou became very upset with her friend and began to shout at her. "I'M NOT MOVING! I'M NOT LETTING ANOTHER CRAZY ASS MAN MAKE ME CHANGE MY LIFE AGAIN! I'M SORRY BUT I AM NOT!"

Bella, not knowing what to say to her friend, agreed with her. "Okay…okay….You win. Then we have to handle this situation ourselves, and I know you did not tell your father what was going on."

Shortly after, Marianne arrived. When she got out of her car she shouted, "SLUMBER PARTY AT LOU'S!"

Lou began to laugh as Bella began to yell at Marianne, "ARE YOU FUCKING CRAZY! SHE HAS A CRAZY NEIGHBOR! Who knows what that person is capable of?"

Lou laughing, watching the two of them going at it, thought it best to shout, "I WILL ORDER PIZZA AND PICK UP BEER!"

Marianne looked over at Bella and said, "Go pack your overnight bag."

Bella, not happy about going to a potentially unsafe location, still agreed to go for her friend's sake. Marianne could tell Bella was not comfortable about going over to Lou's house so she reassured her that there was safety in numbers and that he probably would not do anything knowing that she had company over. Bella, still hesitant, agreed with her friend. She also wanted to be there for Lou.

When the ladies arrived at Lou's they immediately grabbed a beer and headed towards the kitchen window to look for any notes. To their surprise, he did not leave one. It looked as if he was not home at all. All of the lights were out and his car was not in the driveway. All the ladies changed into their pajamas and began to eat pizza.

Bella walked into to Lou's room and came out carrying a little black case. Lou looking at Bella with a smirk on her face asked, "Is that what I think it is?"

Marianne, not having a clue what they were talking about, asked, "What is it?"

Bella opened up the case and looked at Marianne. "Meet Meme, she is my .38 caliber."

Marianne's jaw dropped. "That's a gun. Why would you bring a gun? Are you crazy?!"

Bella and Lou began to laugh. Bella, still laughing, managed, "I don't leave home without her."

Sincerely,

Marianne still not knowing what to say, pleaded, "Please put Meme back in the box. For Christ sake, I don't like guns."

Bella, not wanting her friend to be uncomfortable, put away Meme and placed her under Lou's bed. To make things a little lighter Bella said, "Let's go online to try to find Lou a man."

Marianne got excited. "Yes, let's do it, we can create a profile for you. We can say if you don't mind that your girlfriend can kick your ass then I am the woman for you!"

Lou began laughing and said, "How about...we don't. How about we just get drunk and act stupid." Bella and Marianne agreed. The three ladies stayed up most of the night talking and laughing in spite of everything.

In the morning Lou got up to put the coffee on. When she looked out her window she saw a note on her neighbor's once again. She ran into the bedroom to wake her friends. "Wake up!" she said, "The nut job next door left a note on the damn window again." Marianne and Bella ran past her and straight into the kitchen. When the three of them looked out the window they saw a note that read:

DID YOU AND YOUR FRIENDS HAVE A GOOD
TIME???

Marianne immediately opened the window and yelled, "YES...WE DID HAVE A GOOD TIME,

THANKS FOR ASKING! NOW STOP LEAVING NOTES, YOU'RE KILLING TREES!!!!"

Lou shut the blind in amazement and said, "Where did that come from? You're getting bold in your old age."

Marianne laughed. "Don't fuck with me I'm forty."

Bella, thinking about the note, looked over at her two friends and asked, "How did he know we slept over? He didn't appear to be home when we got here. Do you think he was home the whole time? I mean...he could have parked the car in the garage. He could have been watching us the whole time through the blinds...We never shut your blinds last night."

Not knowing what to say to her friend, Lou tried to dismiss it. "Maybe he was pulling out of his driveway when we were walking in my house. Bella, the guy is just trying to get a rise out of us. I think Marianne's strong words this morning might make him think twice before he kills another tree."

Bella, not happy with Lou's nonchalant way of handling the situation, grabbed her pocketbook and told Lou to call her later. Marianne grabbed her overnight bag, looked at Lou and told her she would call her later.

The next day, Nancy arrived to pick up her daughter. Lou got into the car and the first thing her mother said was, "It's a good day to get new teeth and if you're good I will buy you a coffee after your appointment."

Sincerely,

Lou looked at her mother and just smiled. She was nervous about getting her caps put in.

When they arrived at Dr. Tamin's office the dental assistant called Lou in right away. She could tell Lou was nervous and asked if she wanted the doctor to use nitrous oxide gas. Lou nodded her head yes.

When Dr. Tamin entered the room he looked over at Lou and asked, "Are you nervous about your procedure? This will be a piece of cake I assure you. If you are feeling anxious then I have no problem making you feel comfortable." Lou sighed with relief.

Dr. Tamin explained to her that the gas would just help her relax and that the rest would be a walk in the park. As the doctor started the gas she felt a sense of relaxation that she had not felt in a long time. She began to giggle and asked if she could take the machine home with her. The doctor just laughed and said, "You are not the first patient to ask that."

After Dr. Tamin finished her teeth he went to the waiting room to talk Lou's mother. "Hi, you must be Nancy; Lou told me that you were waiting for her. Everything went great, your daughter was a little nervous so we gave her some nitrous oxide gas. Your daughter is a very funny woman; she must have been very popular in school."

At this Nancy just gave the doctor a strange look. "No, quite the opposite. My daughter always got into fights in school; she always fought for the under-dog. She had a head injury as a child and due to that injury she developed a seizure disorder. She fought her whole life not to be different from everyone else. As an adult she accepts it and tells people it's a blessing."

The doctor became outraged. "She has seizures! She never mentioned that—I gave her gas what if she had a seizure?"

Dr. Tamin stormed into Lou's room. "Did you forget to tell me you have a seizure disorder?"

Lou could tell he was angry. She just looked up at him and answered, "I can tell you have been talking to my mother. Did she mention the fact I have not had one in quite a few years?"

He looked down at her and said, "You still should have mentioned you had a history of seizures, it's nothing to be ashamed of."

Lou got up out of the dentist chair, thanked the doctor for fixing her teeth and walked out. When she arrived back home she went into her bedroom and fell asleep. A few hours later she woke up and on her kitchen table was a coffee and a muffin with a note.

Love, Mom

"Sweet," she thought out loud as she heated up her coffee, grabbed a plate for her muffin, and started her routine. Just as she was about to take a bite of her muffin her cellphone began to ring. It was her father.

"Hey kid, how do you like your new teeth?"

She began to laugh. "I like them."

Michael then went into cop mode. "Hey kid, I did my homework on your client Sarah. She graduated

Sincerely,

college in Tennessee. She comes from a wealthy family, and I can't find anything wrong with her."

Lou with a shocked voice asked, "Really? My gut is telling me different."

Michael became adamant in his response. "*Lisa*, I am telling you I checked this woman out. I cannot find one thing wrong with her. Is there anything you are not telling me?"

Lou, still trusting her gut instinct answered, "No Pop, I gave you everything I had on her and Jack."

Michael wanted to confront his daughter about lying to him for years about what she really did for a living, but he decided it was not the right time. Lou told her father she would call him later, she had to get ready for work.

The following day she received a call from an exuberant Marianne. "Hey Lou, it's the Fall Festival at Slater Park! Do you want to go? My husband and the kids went to his mother's house and I'm bored."

Lou, just wanting to get the hell out of her house, agreed, requesting Marianne pick her up at seven. She told Marianne that she would call Bella to see if she wanted to go. Marianne reminded her that Bella and her husband had gone to Florida to celebrate their anniversary, it would have to be just the two of them.

Chapter 4

THE NIGHT
EVERYTHING CHANGED

Though bummed that Bella would be unable to join them, she still could not wait to get away from her strange neighbor and welcomed the opportunity to escape the craziness. She went to her closet and grabbed a pair of jeans, a black shirt, and wrapped a red and black checkered flannel shirt around her waist. She put on her work boots and headed downstairs to wait for her friend.

When Marianne arrived, Lou was very happy to see her. The first thing Marianne said was, "I am so excited to be going with you to the festival! You haven't been to a festival with me in years!"

When they arrived to Slater Park they could not believe how many cars were in the parking lot. The two ladies headed towards the line. Marianne looked at Lou and said, "Oh we are not standing in line. I or-

Sincerely,

dered the tickets ahead of time so we get to go right to the head of the line."

While standing in line Lou saw her dentist Dr. Tamin and a very attractive blond next to him. She thought to herself, *Of course, a good looking dentist; why not a trophy wife?*

Marianne tapped Lou on the shoulder. "Just to let you know we are going to be part of the first ten people to go in! So get your game face on and remember: it's just people wearing Halloween costumes."

Lou looked at Marianne. "Are you telling me this? Or are you trying to convince yourself? I know you like Halloween. I also know you don't like Halloween masks that cover people's faces! I should be reassuring you!" she said with a laugh.

Marianne rolled eyes at this. "You think you know me."

Lou with a smirk quipped, "I do know you quite well."

Marianne grabbed Lou's arm with excitement. "Look! The creepy guy in the mask is waving for us to go in."

When they went through the gate the first thing they noticed was all the trees were covered with purple LED lights. Some trees had bats hanging from them, others had ghosts. As they continued down the path through the woods they came to a table where two skeletons sat playing cards. All around this display were headstones with different sayings inscribed on them.

They came across a mini cornfield. In front, a skull was resting on a metal post, and just inside there stood a person offering to take pictures of people walking through the haunted path. The two friends agreed to have their picture taken and continued on. Along the path they saw a row of jack-o-lanterns with many elaborate carvings. One featured the mayor of Pawtucket, another McCoy stadium, others Slater Mill and the famous carousel of Slater Park.

At the end of the path there was what looked like a small wooden house with a witch standing in the doorway. A couple in front Marianne and Lou headed towards the little wooden house first, that's when Lou heard the most piercing scream coming from inside. Lou knew by the scream that it was not one of a person who was afraid of someone jumping out from behind a tree. She looked at Marianne and asked her to wait for her.

Lou bolted down the path and saw the woman who was screaming. "THAT'S NOT FAKE...THAT IS NOT FAKE! OH MY GOD, THAT'S SOMEONE'S HEAD!!!"

As Lou approached the table in front of the small wooden house, she ran to see what the woman was pointing at. At that point everything went silent. Lou looked over at the table and stared. She couldn't believe her eyes; her heart began to beat fast as she dropped to her knees and began to scream. "THIS IS MY FAULT! OH MY GOD! THIS IS MY FAULT!"

Lou's whole body began to shake as she looked up at the table one more time and saw the de-

Sincerely,

capitated head of her best friend Bella and her husband. Both of them had their teeth removed and a small
candle placed on their tongues.

Marianne could hear Lou screaming and began
to run towards her friend. Lou jumped up off the
ground and shouted for Marianne to stay where she
was. Marianne ignored her and ran towards the table.
She began to scream and cry as she looked at her
childhood friend's head resting on the table, a skele-
ton's hand atop it. Lou grabbed her friend and began to
hug her. She looked at the table one more time and noticed a note next to Bella's husband's head. It simply
read:

Sincerely,

With tears rolling down her face, Lou felt her
heart being filled with grief and hatred. She wanted to
scream! She released Marianne from her protective
embrace and told her friend to stay where she was, she
would be right back.

Lou began to run down a path. When she got
far enough she whispered, "Why God ? Why? I can't
take anymore, I am dying inside. Please Lord! Help!"

Lou began taking her rage out on a nearby tree.
She was punching the tree and she could feel the purple LED lights going into her hand. She kept thinking
about what Jack did to her and now her best friend was
dead. She began to punch the tree harder and harder,
not realizing that her knuckles were split open and
bleeding.

She finally stopped when she heard the leaves rustling behind her. She knew she was not alone on the haunted path. She placed her hand in her pocket and pulled out her keys and grabbed her mace, finger on the nozzle ready to spray.

She heard a familiar voice. "Lisa, it's Dad."

She ran into her father's arms and began to cry. "Pop this is my fault! Bella and Bill are dead. I was following Sincerely in Texas. I'm sorry Pop, I lied to you."

Michael held his daughter tight. "We will talk about that later, right now I need to get you and Marianne out of here."

Michael walked his daughter over to the cruiser where Marianne was waiting. When Lou got into the cruiser she saw that her friend was inconsolable. She opened the door and sat in the back seat with her friend. Marianne began to yell at Lou, "Don't you ever leave me like that again. I was afraid...I was scared, and you left me."

Lou's eyes filled with tears. "I am so sorry; I will never do that to you again. Please forgive me." The two friends hugged as the police cruiser left to take them down to the station.

When they arrived, Lou and Marianne were led into a room to go over any information they might know regarding the murder of their friend. Marianne explained to the police that she thought her friend Bella and her husband Bill were in Florida celebrating their anniversary.

Sincerely,

Michael entered the room carrying coffees for the two ladies. He let Marianne know that her husband was on his way. He looked over to his daughter and asked her to follow him to his office. When Lou entered her father's office he pulled out a first aid kit and began to wrap his daughter's hand with an ace bandage. She looked up at her father and began to tell him about how she lied to him all these years about what she did for a living. She then proceeded to discuss how she got involved in the Sincerely case.

"Pop, it was about a year ago when a detective from the Texas police approached me about a case he called the Sincerely Case. He wanted me to be a second set of eyes. There had been multiple murders of different people who had very good backgrounds. All the victims' heads were left in various locations, all the victims' teeth were removed. When I started to do my investigation, I discovered there were other murders in different states with the same M.O. All the victims' heads were left, and teeth removed. The murderer always left a note on a white piece of paper typed with an old-school typewriter. Sincerely. Just sincerely. I do have my files in my storage unit; I use it as an office."

Michael looked at his daughter. "Tomorrow we are going to your so-called office and you are going to get me everything you have on him. Do you understand me?"

Lou put her head down as if she were a little girl again. "Yes Pop."

Just then there was a knock on the door. It was an officer letting Michael and Lou know that Marianne's husband had arrived. When Lou walked out into the hallway she saw Marianne hugging her husband. Marianne's husband withdrew from the embrace and went walking over to Lou with an enraged look on his face.

He began to shout. "Stay the hell away from my wife. Your career choice is why Bella and Bill are dead. Are you fucking happy now? I won't let you endanger my wife."

Lou's eyes began to fill up with tears as she looked over at her best friend, her heart breaking. "He's right, it's better that we don't talk or see each other anymore. I could never live with myself if something happened to you too."

Marianne looked at her husband and Lou with tears pouring down her face. "Both of you listen to me...I have just had one of the worst moments of my life. I don't know how I feel or what I am supposed to think right now. What I do know is that I am not going to stay away from Lou." Lou started to interrupt her friend but Marianne quickly snapped, "Shut up and listen to what I have to say. We have been friends since we were eight years old Lou, blood sisters, remember? Remember we were in my backyard and I fell onto a piece of glass and cut my hand. We became blood sisters."

Lou flashed back to that day. The two of them were playing baseball in her backyard. Marianne was running towards home plate when she tripped and cut herself on a piece of glass. When she stood up she was bleeding with glass sticking out of her hand. Lou removed the glass from her hand and cut her own hand. She grabbed Marianne's bloody hand and said, "We are now blood sisters."

Marianne walked over to her to friend, grabbed her hand and showed her matching scar. "I will call you tomorrow and we will figure this out, together." Lou nodded her head.

Michael walked over to his daughter. "Let's get out of here kid, I'm going to take you home. You will have a couple of unmarked vehicles parked outside your house for the night. I will be doing a walkthrough of your apartment when we get there."

When they arrived at her apartment her father did the walkthrough and everything appeared to fine. He looked at his daughter and kissed her on the cheek saying, "You have enough people outside watching this apartment; you will be safe. If you want me to stay I will stay."

Lou hugged her father. "I just want to be alone right now...I love you Pop." He kissed her cheek and said goodbye.

After her father left she went into her room and grabbed her grey sweatpants and a white T-shirt, then went to take a shower. While in the shower she began to cry. She could not get the image of her best friend Bella and Bill out of her head. She felt the anger building up inside of her again. Her world was coming down around her. In her mind she blamed herself for the deaths of her friends. She thought to herself if she had never come back to Rhode Island, her friends would still be alive.

She left the shower and got dressed, went to the kitchen and grabbed herself a beer. She walked into her bedroom, stood in front of her crucifix, and began to pray. Praying for God to take the anger out of her heart, she begged God to forgive her for the deaths of her friends.

Unbeknownst to her, the neighbor was watching her from the window. As he stood in the window watching her pray, he began to wonder what she was praying for.

Is she praying for a man? He began to laugh to himself thinking out loud, "Lord knows you never see one coming or going. Maybe she's praying to her God to get a life and stop being such a bitch."

He yelled, "Maybe your God thinks you're a fucking loser, maybe you should be praying to get a life." He continued watching her as she stood in front of the crucifix crying and he began to mock her "Boo Hoo, oh you're fucking killing me with all this crying. I've had enough, I'm going to bed."

As he walked to his room to call it a night he began to wonder if his opinion of her might be wrong.

Lou knew she would not be able to sleep that night so she decided to put on a baseball hat and baggy sweatshirt to sneak out of the apartment without the police outside noticing her. She decided to go through the bulkhead in the basement and out the back. The storage unit was not a far jog from there.

When she arrived she put the light on and locked the door behind her. She immediately opened

Sincerely,

her box marked "Sincerely." She wrote down all the victims' names and noticed the killings began in Tennessee. She began to wonder why he removed the teeth. At first she thought the most logical explanation was that there would be no dental records, but all the victims' names were under Missing Persons.

While going through the files she found a copy of a Sincerely note. She knew it was from an old-school typewriter. She thought she would take the paper with her to a couple of antique dealers, and perhaps they could tell her the make and model of the typewriter. She took the list of names and the photocopy, placed them in her pocket, and then headed back home.

When she arrived and snuck back in unnoticed, she grabbed her pajamas and went to grab her slippers. As she bent down she noticed Bella's gun case under the bed. She looked up and smiled and said, "Thank you Bella."

The next morning she got up to make herself a cup of coffee and realized she was out. She grabbed her keys to go grab a coffee. When she went out to the garage she noticed her garage window was open. She also noticed her car was covered with newspaper. When she looked closely, it was a picture of her kneeling down in front of Bella's head at Slater Park. She began to rip the newspaper off her car. As soon as she ripped off the last piece, she ran upstairs, opened her kitchen window, and began to yell as loud as she could, "FUCK OFF AND LEAVE ME THE FUCK ALONE! I'VE BEEN THROUGH ENOUGH!"

Lou heard banging at the door. She ran to it quickly and when she opened it she saw it was her father, gun drawn. "Who the hell are you yelling at? Is someone in this house?"

Lou shouted, "Pop put the gun away! I'm just yelling at my stupid neighbor."

Michael with a puzzled look on his face asked, "Why are you yelling at your neighbor?"

She didn't know what to say so she answered the best way she knew how. "His guest was blocking my driveway."

He just looked at Lou and thought, *Does this kid ever know how to tell me the truth?* Standing behind her father were two officers. "Lou, these gentleman are here to set up security cameras, you and I are going to your storage unit."

When they arrived at Lou's storage unit he could not believe how she had it set up. As he looked around he noticed an apartment-size fridge. He looked at his daughter and asked, "Do I dare ask what you have in the fridge?"

Lou just looked up from the Sincerely box and said, "A used condom."

Her father just stood and stared at her. "You are a nut," he replied.

Lou just started laughing. She then went into work mode. "Pop, I have the files we need. Did you get anything from the security cameras at the park? How about any witnesses?"

Michael, impressed with his daughter said, "No, not yet. They are going through it as we speak.

Sincerely,

Lou, how are you doing? It broke my heart to see you and Marianne so devastated."

Before he could say another word Lou changed the subject. "Then help me catch the son of a bitch who killed my friends." She stood up with hate in her eyes. "Either you help me or I will do this myself, but either way I am going after him."

Before Michael could comment, his cellphone began to ring; it was a fellow officer telling Michael to get to the Wreath Side Cemetery. He hung up the phone. "We have to go now."

Lou could tell by her father's face something was up. As they pulled up to the cemetery Michael and Lou had no idea what they were walking into. The first thing Lou noticed was caution tape surrounding two gravesites. As she walked closer her heart began to beat fast. She was wondering who the hell was in the graves. An officer met the two of them.

"Chief, this is the most fucked up thing I've ever seen."

Michael walked over. He looked over at Lou, not knowing how to tell her what he just saw. She ran over to the gravesites and when she looked inside it was the headless bodies of Bella and Bill. Both had headstones. The first one read, "Bella Matick loving wife," the second one read, "William Matick beloved husband."

Lou's eyes began to fill up. She could hear her father's voice trying to ask her questions but the only thing she could do was just stare into the graves.

Finally, Michael grabbed Lou. "I need you to concentrate for one minute. I know this is a lot to take in, but I need you to listen to me."

She looked at her father and all she wanted to do was scream. She did her best to keep it together.

"*Lisa* listen to me, has Sincerely ever done this before? Has he ever put his victims in a grave before?"

She looked at her father. "No, none of the bodies were ever found."

Michael, trying to stay in cop mode and not dad mode, began to question his daughter as if she was any civilian. "I think what he did was personal, he wanted you to know he was here. He knows who you are, but showed you respect by burying the bodies and leaving the headstones."

She became outraged. "Respect, he killed my best friend and her husband. I should have never listened to you and Mom! I should have stayed in Texas!"

Michael, trying not to get upset with his daughter, said, "Listen, this is good. This means he respects you, if he respects you he will make a mistake." She knew her father was right. She just wanted to leave the cemetery and go home.

When they arrived back at Lou's apartment Michael asked Lou if there was anything he could do for her. She asked him to make sure that Marianne and her family were safe.

Michael just smiled. "I already have. Marianne's husband and kids are long gone and far away from Rhode Island."

Sincerely,

Lou was puzzled by her father's response and asked, "What about Marianne? Is she okay?"

Michael just smiled again. "Let's just say I know why the two of you have been friends for so long."

There was a knock on her door. Michael opened it, and standing there was Marianne. "Did you really think I would leave you?"

Lou just stood in amazement. "Why are you here? It's not safe!"

Michael intervened. "It would be a lot easier to protect the two of you if you are together. It was not easy convincing Marianne's husband of that."

Michael reminded the two of them that the security cameras were connected to the police department and that there were two unmarked cars just outside. He hugged the two of them and told them he loved them and to call if they needed him.

After he left Lou looked at Marianne. "Beer?"

Marianne blurted out, "I thought you'd never ask!"

Marianne told Lou she heard about what happened in the cemetery. She also told Lou her father's theory about Sincerely respecting her. She then went on to say, "No offense Lou, we've been friends for a long time...I can say that I would not buy you a headstone out of respect. I'm just saying."

Lou began to laugh. "I would buy you one."

Marianne giggled. "That's because we all know you're not right in the head!" Lou then asked Marianne if she wanted some Chinese food for dinner.

After they finished eating, Lou went into her room and pulled out the Sincerely files. She grabbed a piece of poster board and markers. Marianne asked what she was doing.

She replied confidently, "Solving our friend's murder case. Would you like to help?" Marianne asked when the first murder was. Lou pulled out the file and explained, "One of the first victims was in Tellico Plains, Tennessee. The head was found on a popular hiking path. The victim was a male; he was the first with damage to the gums. You could tell by the reports and pictures the teeth were torn out of his mouth while he was alive. Torture, it must have been."

Marianne asked Lou why she thought he was doing this. She had no answer for her friend.

"How old do you think he is?"

Lou shook her head. "I don't know. I'm not a profiler, but if I had to guess I would say mid-forties. I think he's been doing this longer than we think. He now takes his time, in the beginning gums were all torn, now it's like a professional did it and that takes patience. Something a younger person wouldn't have. I just can't figure out why he's doing it."

As the two were reviewing the files, Marianne could picture Bella looking down shaking her head, saying, *Look, I have these two idiots trying to catch my killer.*

She began to laugh out loud. "Hey Lou, how funny would it be if we were actually the ones to catch the killer?"

Sincerely,

Lou, not in the mood for humor, snapped back with a quick answer. "I will catch him. And when I do, I am going to kill him. I want him to suffer the way he made Bella and Bill suffer."

Just then Marianne's cellphone began to ring. It was Bella's sister, Patty.

"Hi Marianne…it's Patty. I just wanted to let you know the wake will be in two days. It will be held at Butterfly Wings Cemetery. Marianne, there is something I have to tell you."

Marianne curiously replied, "What is it Patty?"

Patty's voice began to crack as she spoke. "Were you aware that Bella was sick?"

Confused, Marianne asked, "What do you mean sick?"

Patty began to cry. "My sister had Stage 4 breast cancer. The doctor only gave her four to six months to live. That's why Bill was taking her to Florida. He wanted to have one more vacation with her."

Marianne's eyes began to fill up. She could feel the lump in her throat as she continued to talk with Patty. "Lou and I are devastated about what happened."

Patty was having difficulty speaking. "Words cannot express how I feel about what happened to my sister. When I close my eyes at night I wonder how much she must have suffered. How long did he torture her? Was she screaming for Bill or did she watch Bill die first? I cannot get those thoughts out of my head. I'm sorry Marianne; this is too difficult for me to talk about. See you and Lou at the wake."

When Marianne hung up the phone she began to cry. "Did you know Bella had Stage 4 breast cancer? Our friend was dying and she never told us. Why would she do that? Is it because we were too busy worrying about you and your lousy choice of a career that not only killed our friend but now has me torn away from my family?!"

Lou just sat on the couch, not knowing what to say. She could not believe that her best friend just said that to her. She stood up with tears pouring down her face. "If that's what you think then there's the door. Leave. I didn't ask for any of this. I lost my best friend too. You don't think I am blaming myself for all of this? You don't think I wish I had stayed in Texas so none of you would ever be put in danger? I chose my career and I don't regret it. I do regret that it has now affected everyone I love. It's breaking my heart and I just want to scream. And I can't.

"Do you have any idea what it's like to not show fear? Or to hold your emotions in so people don't think you're a walking basket case? I'm sorry all this has happened, but if you can't handle it leave. You will probably be better off going back with your family."

Marianne just stood silently for a minute. She walked over to her friend and hugged her. "I am so sorry I said those things to you, I didn't mean it. I am just so hurt...and scared Lou. I don't want to leave. I want to stay; I want to help you catch this asshole."

Lou looked at her friend. "I am so sorry. I don't want you to go, I am so sorry that I said that to you."

Sincerely,

Marianne looked at her friend. "I need a beer…and something to eat. This has been the most exhausting night. Of my life."

Lou just laughed, still with tears in her eyes. "I agree."

After the two of them had a couple of beers and something to eat they headed for bed. That night they both stood in front of the crucifix and began to pray together. Unaware the neighbor was watching them.

As the neighbor watched the two friends pray, he began to say, "Oh look, the losers are now praying together, what the hell can they be praying for? Their friend that just died? It was all over the news and newspapers. Get over it, she's gone, you can't bring her back. I never understood the whole praying thing. I know when I was a young boy I used to pray and my prayers were never answered. Let me see if I can remember the prayer I used to say. Oh yeah, I remember now."

"Now I lay me down to sleep,
I pray the Lord, my soul to keep.
If they don't die before I wake.
It is their faces I should Break."

I'm surprised I even remembered that. I'm done watching these whack doodles. I'm going to bed."

Chapter 5

THE CHASE IS ON

It was a wet and somber November day, the day of Bella and Bill's funeral. Marianne and Lou were escorted to the funeral parlor by undercover police officers. When they walked in they saw a video of Bella and Bill on a large screen with photos of the two of them getting married, family holidays, and vacations together. The last photo was a picture of the three friends: Bella, Lou, and Marianne. Lou began to cry, looking over to Marianne. Her heart broke. Marianne was inconsolable as she just stood in front of the screen watching the video with their shared memories, beautiful memories.

Lou approached Marianne and said, "Marianne, take your time. When you're ready we can give our condolences to their families."

Sincerely,

Marianne with tears pouring down her face said, "I'm ready. This is so hard; she has been part of our lives since we were kids."

Lou hugged Marianne. "I know, but right now we need to be strong for Bill and Bella's families."

When Lou and Marianne entered the room, they saw two closed caskets. Together they approached the caskets and knelt before them. Both of them stood up and gave the sign of the cross, walked over to the families and began to give their condolences.

While walking through the line Lou could feel her phone silently vibrating in her purse. She was thinking to herself, *Who the hell could possibly be calling me now? Everyone knows I am here.* As they finished, Lou walked into another room to check her phone. It was the Texas police department.

She answered the phone by saying, "This is not a good time. Is this an emergency?"

It was the captain of the department. "Lou it's Captain Steve Kin. I have something you may be interested in."

She replied inquisitively, "What?"

"We just had a girl who was severely burned in a car accident. She was driving a stolen vehicle, so we had to use dental records to identify the body."

Annoyed, Lou asked, "What does this have to do with me?"

The captain explained, "When the dental records came up, the coroner noticed an implant in the victim's mouth."

"And?"

He continued, "Lou, the number six was engraved into the tooth. When the coroner looked closely at the tooth he had sent to the lab…the tooth was not a porcelain tooth. It was a real one. The tooth was a match for one of our Sincerely victims."

She remained silent for a minute. "Are you telling me that Sincerely implanted his victims' teeth into other people?"

The captain replied, "Yes, the sick motherfucker has not been caught yet! If he's implanting the teeth into other people, he has to be a dentist. We need to go over the files again."

Lou agreed. She explained to the captain that she would contact him when she left the funeral home. Before she hung up the phone she told him she would do some research regarding the implants.

Marianne walked over to Lou. "Who are you talking to? We are at our friend's funeral. What could possibly be that important?"

Lou with a guilty feeling responded, "Marianne, I'm sorry. We have to go."

Marianne became very angry at Lou. "Are you fucking kidding me?! We can't leave; we are at our best friend's funeral for fucks sake!"

Lou in a whisper responded, "I just got a call from a captain of the Texas police department, we may have a break on Sincerely. I need to do some research now. This could be our chance at catching the son of a bitch. Please Marianne, don't be mad."

Sincerely,

Marianne's eyes began to fill up with tears. "You're right; we need to catch the fucker who killed our friend. I just need a minute."

Lou looked at Marianne with sympathy in her eyes. She knew how Marianne loved Bella and this was hard for her. What Marianne did not understand was that Lou was dying inside too. She knew if she showed her emotions that would stop what was really important, which was catching Sincerely. Marianne walked over to the caskets one last time and said her goodbyes to her friends.

Lou walked over to Marianne, gave her a hug and said, "Are you ready to catch this son of a bitch?"

Marianne nodded yes. As they started to leave Michael approached them with a look of concern. "Where are you two going so early in the service?"

Lisa looked at her father. "We may have a lead. I have to go and get some answers."

Michael walked over to his wife Jeannine and told her that he was leaving. She was not happy, but she understood the work her husband did. Michael caught up to Lou and Marianne and said, "Let's go. What do you need from my department?"

When the three of them got into his car, she told her father about the phone call she had just received. She looked at her father and asked, "Can we go back to my house? I have all my files and my computer."

Michael agreed. When they arrived at her house she looked at her father and said, "Why do you think he's implanting the teeth? Why not throw them away? Who in their right fucking mind would do that?"

Michael smiled at Lou and replied, "We need to find him to ask him."

"If or when we catch him, trust me, there will not be a lot of talking."

Marianne also chimed in, " The only thing I want to know...why Bella? Do you think he knew she was sick? Do you think he was trying to spare her from what she was going to go through with the cancer?"

Michael was confused. "What do you mean cancer? Did Bella have cancer?"

Lou's eyes began to fill up with tears. "Yes Pop, we found out a couple of days ago. Her sister called and told us."

Michael started after some thought, "Kid if this is true, then maybe in his sick way he thought he was saving you the grief. I'm telling you kid, for some reason this guy is showing you respect. He is going to fuck up soon. He is showing signs of weakness and it's for you."

Lou felt that anger building up again. "I don't need or want his respect. I want him dead for what he has done to my friends. Pop, please help me catch him."

Michael hugged his daughter and kissed her on the head saying, "I don't know if you are in any shape to be doing this right now. Too much emotion running through you and you're too tied to the case."

She became angry and shouted, "DON'T TELL ME WHAT I AM, OR WHAT I AM NOT SUPPOSED

Sincerely,

TO BE! I AM PISSED OFF AND I HAVE THAT RIGHT! I HAVE THE RIGHT TO FEEL THE WAY I DO! DO NOT TELL ME I AM TOO ATTACHED! I AM GOING TO CATCH THIS MOTHERFUCKER WITH YOU OR WITHOUT YOU!"

Marianne looked at Michael and said, "I am with her, I am going to back her no matter how crazy her decision making is."

Lou softened at these words looking at Marianne. "Thank you my friend."

Michael looked at the two girls and smiled. "Okay where do you want to start?"

Lou looked at her father. "I am going to call my dentist tomorrow to get information on how Sincerely could possibly transplant the teeth of his victims into his patients."

The next morning Lou got up early and made coffee for Marianne and started on breakfast. She could hear Marianne enter the kitchen. "I just got off the phone with my husband. He wanted me to tell you to be careful and to take care of me."

Lou smiled. "Of course I will." She continued to cook breakfast and thought about how she asked God to keep Marianne safe so she could return back to her family.

Marianne walked over to the kitchen window. "Hey Lou, have you had any more notes from your crazy neighbor lately?"

Lou shook her head. "No, the last thing he did was post the newspaper article of you and me on my car. I think he's finally got the hint that I really don't give a shit."

Marianne looked at Lou with a shit eating grin. "Maybe he had a crush on you."

Lou laughed, "Maybe he's just a nut job who lives next door."

Marianne after some silence asked, "What are the chances that you would have two crazy people in your life at once?"

Lou grinned. "Make that three, did you forget about Jack Coral?"

Marianne put her head down. "I totally forgot about him! With everything that's going on with Sincerely—I am so sorry I forgot the man who almost killed you. How the hell do you sleep at night?"

Lou started to laugh. "I pretend that this is not my life, and I dream of myself living at a lake house, standing on a dock drinking a coffee."

Marianne smiled. "Someday you will have your lake house, and your dock."

Lou walked into her bedroom to call Dr. Tamin to ask him if she could meet with him. After her call to the dentist's office she walked into the living room and told Marianne to get ready, the dentist would meet with them at noon. Marianne headed to the bedroom to get ready and asked Lou if they could go walking through Lincoln Woods when they finished their meeting with Dr. Tamin. Lou liked the idea and reminded Marianne that the undercover police would be following them the whole time.

Marianne laughed, "I hope they can keep up."

Sincerely,

Lou started laughing.

When they arrived at Dr. Tamin's office the secretary led them inside. He stood up from his chair, shook their hands, and started the conversation by saying, "Well, Lisa—I'm sorry, Lou—could you please explain what the emergency was that you had to come to my office? Are you having an issue with your teeth?"

She looked at Dr. Tamin and said, "No, the teeth are fine. I just have a very strange question to ask you."

Dr. Tamin peered at her with a very curious look. "What would you like to ask me?"

She took a deep breath and asked, "Is it possible to use a human tooth for an implant or cap? I know this sounds like a crazy question, but I just need to know if it can be done."

Dr. Tamin looked at Lou with confusion prominent on his face. "Why on earth would you want to know something like that?"

Marianne at that point intervened. "We had a bet! I said that no one could ever do such a procedure; Lou said it could be done. We have a fifty dollar bet on this."

Dr. Tamin had a look of anger on his face. "You wasted my time...came to settle a bet! Do you have any idea how busy I am? Please leave."

Embarrassed, Lou stood up and said, "I'm sorry, I cannot get into the details. I just need to know if it is possible; can you please tell me?"

Dr. Tamin angrily responded, "Anything is possible. My concern would be infection developing in the gum tissue. Did I answer your question?"

Lou extended her hand for a shake. "Yes, sorry for wasting your time."

The doctor shook her hand and had his assistant walk them out. As Lou and Marianne were walking to the car Marianne whispered, "That did not go so well."

Lou grinned. "Really? You had to say we were having a bet."

Marianne giggled. "I got nervous…it's the first thing that came to my head. No offense, he did not seem overly impressed that we took time out of his schedule to ask what sounds like a crazy question. We sound nuts."

Lou agreed. "Let's go walking, I need to de-stress."

The two ladies arrived at Lincoln Woods to start their hike. Following them were the plainclothes police officers. While walking they took in how beautiful Lincoln Woods looked with all the foliage turning yellow and orange.

As they were enjoying the smell of the crisp fall air, Lou's cellphone began to ring. Her father wanted an update. "Hi kid, what did the dentist say?"

Lou replied, "Not much, he said anything is possible."

Michael let her know that he'd requested a list of all the dentists in Tennessee and Texas. He also let

Sincerely,

her know that the Texas Police Department was working with him to go through the list.

She thanked her father for helping her with the case; she had a sense of security knowing he was going to be by her side. As they continued walking through Lincoln Woods, Lou asked Marianne if she wanted to walk to the lake, a big part of these woods. When they finally arrived they climbed up on one of the lifeguard chairs and the two ladies started to reminisce about all the good times they had coming to the lake.

Lou looked at Marianne. "Do you ever miss how things used to be? I mean, nowadays all I see are kids talking on cellphones or playing video games. You hardly ever see kids in the streets playing like we used to. When we were kids we were never home...unless we were grounded of course."

Marianne responded, "Do you remember how all the kids in the neighborhood would play manhunt, kickball, or have slumber parties? We'd be watching scary movies and eating popcorn. Everything was simple."

Lou added to Marianne's comment, "I think kids today are growing up so fast that they are forgetting the most important thing in life, which is to enjoy being a kid. Growing up is not all it's cracked up to be." She laughed. She asked Marianne if she was ready to head back to the house and possibly wanted a coffee. Marianne quickly nodded yes.

Marianne was thinking how this day felt like a normal day; just two friends hanging out, no crazy people trying to kill you. She was also thinking about how much she missed her husband and kids and how she wished the insanity would all end soon.

When they arrived to the house Lou and Marianne stood in the kitchen trying to figure out what their next move was going to be. Marianne decided to sit down at the table. but when she turned to look out of the window she noticed a note. "Looks like your crazy neighbor is at it again."

Lou rolled her eyes and said, "What did the crazy ass say now?"

Marianne began to read the note aloud:

I'VE ENJOYED BEING YOUR Neighbor,
SINCERELY

Lou dropped the mug of coffee she was holding out of her hands. She screamed for Marianne to move away from the window.

Marianne screamed, "Oh MY GOD, HE'S BEEN LIVING NEXT DOOR THE WHOLE FUCK-ING TIME!"

Lou ran to her room and grabbed Bella's gun. Marianne grabbed her cellphone and called Michael as fast as her fingers could dial him. He answered and she blurted out in a panic, "Sincerely has been living next door to us the whole time!"

He yelled into the phone, "What?! What are you saying?! Are kidding me?! Where is Lou?!"

Marianne could feel her body start to shake with fear as she answered him. "She's just run into the

Sincerely,

bedroom—hold on she's heading out of the door with Bella's gun!"

Lou yelled, "Let's go!"

Michael began to yell at Marianne on the phone, "DO NOT LET HER LEAVE THAT HOUSE!"

Marianne responded, "I'm sorry, I'm not letting her go by herself." Marianne hung up the phone and followed her friend.

Michael contacted the undercover police outside of the apartment and informed them not to let them near that house until backup arrived. As the girls ran towards the house, they were stopped by the cops. "Sorry ladies, strict orders that you are not allowed in the house."

Lou could hear sirens approaching and sure enough, within a matter of minutes the neighborhood was surrounded by police.

Her father got out of the police car, looked at her, and yelled, "Wait here until I call for you!"

She became angry and yelled back at her father, "NO! That motherfucker killed my friend! I'm going in with you!"

Michael yelled back, "Get it through your fucking head, you're not going into that house until I tell you!" He yelled to the officers to escort Lou and Marianne back to her apartment.

When she was back inside Lou ran to her bedroom window to see if she could hear anything coming from next door. She could hear the police yelling from room to room, "Clear." Her heart was racing; she was praying he was in the house so this nightmare would be over, so she could face him. She needed to face him.

A half hour passed and her cellphone rang. It was her father saying, "I need you and Marianne to come to the house." Lou asked Marianne if she was ready to go next door.

Marianne was nervous but did not want Lou to know. Her voice began to crack and she nodded her head yes.

Lou knew her friend was afraid of what they were going to see. She grabbed Marianne by the hand. "Let's go, we can do this."

The two walked to the house, both afraid of what they were going to see. Her father was waiting at the door and handed them each a pair of latex gloves to wear before entering the house. As they entered, Marianne could not believe how clean and decorated it was, with high-end furniture and paintings that could fetch quite a price. Marianne looked at Lou before saying, "Well, this is not what I expected... If this is the case I'm going to become a serial killer."

Lou looked at Marianne. "Really?"

Michael asked the ladies to follow him up the stairs. Going up the staircase, all Lou could see were the police taking pictures and dusting for fingerprints. When they made it to the top of the stairs he led the two ladies to Sincerely's bedroom.

The first thing they noticed was a wall of pictures of Lou, Marianne, and Bella. The first picture Lou noticed was one of her crying in her kitchen when Bella died. Marianne noticed a picture of the three

Sincerely,

friends out for drinks and another of the three of them in Lou's kitchen. Lou then noticed a picture of her discovering Bella and Bill's heads at Slater Park. Marianne grabbed her arm. "That's you praying in your fucking bedroom! He has taken like ten pictures of you praying!"

Michael walked over to Lou and handed her a picture. She snatched it from his hand. When she looked at the picture her hands began to shake. "He took a picture of me in the hospital after Jack Coral attacked me. What the *fuck* is going on?"

He hugged her and said, "I promise we will catch him."

Marianne asked Michael, "Are you finding anything in this house that will lead us to him?"

Just then they heard an officer yell, "CHIEF, COME DOWN TO THE BASEMENT! WE FOUND SOMETHING."

The ladies followed him down to the basement. They could smell a strong odor. Lou covered her nose. Immediately she knew what the smell was. She was just waiting to see who it was. At one end of the basement the officer found a door that was hidden behind the entertainment center. Inside the room was the head of man with no teeth placed on a bucket. When Lou approached the head she knew it was her original neighbor. Next to her neighbor's head she noticed an envelope taped to the wall, addressed to her.

Michael looked at her and asked, "What is it?"

Lou asked for an evidence bag as she gently removed the tape and placed the envelope in the bag.

When she turned to Marianne, her friend looked ready to be sick. "Are you ok? You don't look so good."

Marianne, with a decidedly pale complexion, looked at Lou and said, "I'm fffiii—" She could not even finish the word before she began to vomit all over the floor.

Lou ran over to her friend and held her hair as she violently emptied her stomach. Michael ran over and grabbed an empty box so Marianne could finish. One of the officers placed some trash bags on the floor to prevent more evidence from being destroyed. Marianne lifted her head from the box and began to cry. "I just want to go home. I want my husband and kids. This is too much for me to handle. Please Lou, I need to go home."

Lou hugged her friend. "I promise you, you will go home soon. I am done being his victim."

Michael had one of the officers take them back to Lou's apartment. He told Lou he was going to take the letter to the station and he would meet them back at her apartment later. When he arrived at the Pawtucket Police Department he took the letter to forensics. As they opened the letter to see what Sincerely left for Lou, he became anxious. He was thinking what this sick fuck could possibly write to his daughter. Was he going to threaten to kill her or her friend Marianne? Was he going to be waiting in the dark, waiting to take her and torture her?

The forensics officer opened the letter and looked at Michael before saying, "It's addressed to you."

Sincerely,

With a puzzled look on his face Michael said, "What do you mean it's for me?" He grabbed the letter and began to read it:

Dear Michael,

Did you really think I was going to leave a letter for your daughter so you could read it? As much as I enjoy watching you try to protect your daughter, the fact is you cannot protect her from me. I can be anywhere at any time and I have proved that time and time again. Good luck Pop.

Sincerely

Michael punched the wall and yelled, "I WANT HIM DEAD, DEAD NOT ARRESTED, DEAD! THAT SCUMBAG PIECE OF SHIT!"

He walked out of the forensics office and went to his personal office. He opened his desk drawer and poured himself a glass of vodka. As he drank he was trying to think of how he was going to tell his daughter about the letter, or *if* he was going to tell her at all. He just kept thinking on repeat, *She has been through so much, how much more can she take before she breaks?* As he sat with his thoughts, something came over him. He realized that Sincerely did leave a note for Lou, it just wasn't that letter. Michael grabbed his keys and headed straight back to Sincerely's house.

Back at Lou's apartment she asked Marianne if she wanted a beer. Marianne asked if she had anything stronger.

"Yes, I have some tequila. Would you like a shot?"

"Hell yes."

She asked Marianne if she was up for a shot considering she had just vomited. Marianne reassured her that her vomiting was a combination of her smelling the decaying head and her nerves. Lou opened her hutch and grabbed the tequila and two shots glasses. As they sat in the living room taking shots the doorbell rang. Lou thought it had to be her father, though he usually called first when he was on his way over.

As she looked out the living room window she saw a pizza delivery car. She thought to herself, *My father must have ordered us pizza for dinner.* She went into her room, grabbed her mace and headed down the stairs. When she opened the door the delivery man handed her the pizza and told her to have a good evening.

As the delivery man was about to walk away she asked him, "But…how much do I owe you?"

He turned and shrugged. "Nothing, your order was already paid for."

Lou became very suspicious and asked, "Who ordered the pizza?"

The delivery guy, becoming agitated with her, yelled, "LISTEN LADY I ONLY DELIVER THE SHIT! I DON'T ASK WHO! WHAT! WHERE! WHEN! OR HOW! DO YOU WANT THE PIZZA OR NOT?!"

Lou yelled back, "ASSHOLE I WILL TAKE THE FUCKING PIZZA! MAYBE YOU SHOULD

Sincerely,

PICK ANOTHER CAREER!" The delivery man got into his car and gave her the middle finger before driving away.

She brought the pizza upstairs and placed it on the dining room table. She looked at Marianne and said, "I don't think the pizza delivery guy will ever deliver here again."

Marianne smiled. "Do I dare ask why?"

"No." Lou grabbed two plates and brought them into the dining room.

When Marianne opened the pizza box she noticed an envelope taped to the inside of the lid. She carefully removed the envelope from the box and handed it to Lou. "Here …I think this is for you."

As Lou grabbed the note from Marianne she became apprehensive about what could possibly be inside the envelope. Marianne asked her if they should call her father first. Lou paused for a moment but nodded her head no. She opened the envelope and it was a letter from Sincerely:

My Dearest Lou,

This is my letter to say good-bye… for now. I have come to the conclusion that you are not the person I thought you were. You are not the narcissistic person I thought you might be. Instead you are a person who shows kindness and empathy towards people. Which is something I very rarely come across. You and Marianne have a true friendship…one that is made from love and a respect for one another. This gives me hope that not everyone is a scumbag piece of shit. I am

96

not going to come for you or Marianne...at this time. I still have more business to attend to. I am only up to 36 victims you know, I have not met my goal. When I do finish my work I will come for you, you will be my masterpiece. People will talk about your murder for generations.

Until we meet again,
Sincerely

Lou ripped the note as an overwhelming feeling of anger rose up in her. She began to yell, "Masterpiece, you think we are going to be your masterpiece?! I will kill you first, I swear to God!"

Marianne stood in silence as she was thinking to herself, *This is never going to end. I am never going to be with my family again.* She knew at this point there would be no way out of this situation unless she or Sincerely died. Marianne, with tears in her eyes, walked over to the tequila bottle, grabbed a couple shot glasses, and poured two shots, handing Lou one. The two stood in silence and drank.

Marianne, the tears steadily pouring down her face, looked at her best friend and said, "I love you, but I need to get back to my family. I think it's time we take matters into our own hands and kill this motherfucker."

Lou grabbed the tequila and poured two more shots before looking at her friend and saying, "I promise you, you will be back with your family, and if it means us killing him then so be it."

Sincerely,

Marianne asked, "How do we get started? We don't even know who he is!"

Lou thought for a minute. "We do have something. I have his sperm."

Marianne started to giggle. "Well that's a first."

Lou began to laugh. "Remember when he left the condom on the wine bottle? I kept it. Something told me to keep it so I did."

Marianne was both happy to hear her friend had the sperm and concerned that she kept it. "How are we going to get the sperm tested? Are you going to ask your father to have it tested?"

"No. I am going to call Joanne in Tennessee to have it tested. I think Sincerely expects us to keep using the Pawtucket Police Department. It's time we think outside the box like him. Where's my phone? I will call Jo now and see how we can do this."

Still as brilliant as when she was in school with Lou, Bella, and Marianne, Joanne had risen to a high position in a Tennessee hospital. As a prestigious doctor of internal medicine, Joanne had access to the resources to get the sperm tested. As Lou's still close friend, Joanne would hopefully be willing to bend the rules for her.

Lou called her friend Joanne, knowing she had a lot of explaining to do.

After telling her everything, Joanne responded, "Why did you wait so long to call me? Never mind, that's not important right now. What you are going to do is place the sperm in some dry ice and send it to the hospital I work at and send it priority mail. Once I have it I will send it to the lab. The only way this will work is if he is already in the Combined DNA System Index. For your sake I hope that he is."

Lou thanked her friend and told her she would send it the following day.

The next day Lou went to the local fish market and asked the owner for some dry ice and packaging for a fish order she wanted to send. The owner looked at Lou like she had five heads. "Do you want fish with the packaging or do you plan on buying the fish elsewhere?"

She laughed. "I meant I am sending my brother lobster! Could you please package it for me to ship?"

The owner offered to ship it for her but she told him that she was shipping other items with it.

When she arrived back at the apartment she was greeted by Marianne and her father. Michael asked her what she had gotten at the seafood store. She replied, "I was craving lobster so I thought Marianne and I could have that for dinner."

Michael looked at Lou, puzzled, and asked, "Why do you have it packaged?"

Lou laughed. "Pop, I was going to mail Shane some lobsters for his birthday, but when I called Mom and told her what I just bought for Shane she reminded me that he was coming home for his birthday."

Michael stood and looked at his daughter for a minute before saying, "Is this the story you want me to believe?"

Lou looked at her father and said, "Yes, this *is* the story I need you to believe for now."

Sincerely,

He began to yell. "DO YOU THINK THIS IS A FUCKING GAME?! THIS GUY WANTS YOU AND MARIANNE DEAD! FIRST YOU LIED TO ME ABOUT WHAT YOU DID FOR A LIVING AND I FIND OUT THE NIGHT YOU WERE ALMOST KILLED! NOW YOU HAVE SOME OTHER FUCKING PSYCHO TRY-ING TO KILL YOU! HOW MUCH MORE DO YOU THINK I CAN TAKE?!"

Lou's eyes began to fill up with tears. "Pop, I am so sorry for everything I put you through, but you need to trust me. I have a lead but the less people who know the better. I promise you, when I find out any-thing I will let you know. I love you Pop, more than words can say. I will not do anything that will put Ma-rianne or myself in danger."

He hugged his daughter and let her know that he could not survive if anything happened to her or any of his children. She looked up at her father and asked why he was over. Michael asked Marianne and Lou to sit down before explaining. "Okay ladies, we found out another way Sincerely has been hiding his evidence."

Marianne looked puzzled and asked, "Do you mean other than in his patients?"

He answered, "No, he is still implanting the teeth of his victims in patients, but a prisoner in a Ken-tucky prison had one of the teeth implanted in his mouth. According to the Kentucky Police Department a prisoner was having difficulty from dental work he had done over a year ago. When the new dentist went to check out what the issue was he came across the implant that Sincerely had placed in the prisoner. The

100

tooth was numbered eighteen. They are now trying to check the DNA for the tooth."

Marianne with enthusiasm in her voice said, "Then we finally know who he is? Did they tell you the name of the dentist?"

Michael answered, "From what they told me his name is Dr. A. Blackstone. I am waiting for them to send me a picture of him."

Marianne asked how they would have a picture. He explained that any medical personnel who worked in a prison would have to have a picture ID. Lou asked how long it would take for the picture of Dr. Blackstone to come in. He told her when he received the photo he would let her know. Michael stood up and told the girls he was going to leave, but before he left he asked Lou to let him know what she found out with whatever she was hiding from him. She gave her word to her father, gave him a hug, and he left.

After Michael drove away Marianne went to the fridge and grabbed Sincerely's condom. Lou removed the lobsters and placed them in the fridge. She then placed the condom in an evidence bag and placed it in the dry ice and sealed the package. The two ladies then rushed to the post office to have it sent overnight.

Two weeks went by before Lou finally received a phone call from her friend Joanne. "Hi Jo, please tell me you have some news for me."

Joanne immediately began to tell Lou what she found out. "Lou you lucked out, his name was on file! His name is Bradley Forest Elmwood, he is from Tennessee."

Sincerely,

"Are you fucking kidding me?"

"Wait, it gets better. When Bradley was nineteen he was accused of sexually assaulting a woman who he had met at a local bar near the college he was attending." Lou asked if he was arrested for the assault.

Joanne answered, "No, according to my coworker who remembers the story, he was cleared of all charges. He admitted to having sex with the woman and the case was dropped. According to my sources Bradley comes from a very wealthy family. His father was the governor of Tennessee for two terms and he was going to run for president but his wife took sick. Rumor has it she had a nervous breakdown and now lives in an assisted living facility for people with mental illness."

Lou then asked Joanne if she was up for some visitors from back home. Joanne laughed and replied, "I already set up my spare rooms for you and Marianne. When will I be expecting you?"

Lou told Joanne within the next couple of days. She let Joanne know that it would not be easy for her to get out of Pawtucket without her father knowing and thanked her for all her help.

Chapter 6

SINCERELY IN THE MAKING

Bradley Forest Elmwood was born to Evelyn Forest and James Elmwood. He grew up in Belle Meade, Tennessee, a very affluent neighborhood. Evelyn was a gynecologist, and a loving wife and mother. James followed in the steps of his grandfather and father and chose a career in government. James was a "no nonsense" individual who demanded perfection and aspired to have the perfect wife and child.

Growing up, Bradley did better educationally than most of the students in his class. He had very few friends and for the most part kept to himself. One day when he was in fifth grade he brought his report card home and was proud of the grades he made and excited to show his father. He ran to his father's office to show him his report card and James looked at the grades

Sincerely,

with a smile on his face. When he glanced over at the physical education grade Bradley received a C+.

James looked at the C+ with disgust and said, "What kind of fucking pussy gets C+ in gym? You are an Elmwood; you should be getting an A in Physical Education. How the hell did you get a C+ in gym?"

Bradley's heart sank and with tears in eyes replied he stuttered, "I just...I...don't like taking gym. I'd rather go to the library and read." Bradley did not want to tell him that some of the kids in the class made fun of him because of the stories of his father's "political" escapades they heard from their parents.

Evelyn heard her husband raising his voice at Bradley. When she entered James's office, she could see the tears pouring down Bradley's face. She looked at James and yelled sharply, "What did you say to him?!"

James rolled his eye and snapped back condescendingly, "Your pussy of a son got a C+ in gym—he claims he'd rather go to the library."

Evelyn, disgusted by her husband's reaction to Bradley's report card, responded, "Your son is a straight A student James, who never gets in trouble in school and you have the audacity to put him down for getting a C+ in gym? Maybe you should look in a mirror; you're not the jock you used to be when we dated in college."

She grabbed Bradley by the hand and they left James's office. Evelyn looked at Bradley and told him she was proud of him and that he should become anything he wanted to be in life and not what the family wanted him to be. She wiped away his tears and kissed him on the forehead and asked him to get ready for supper.

Before walking away he asked, "Mom…why do you love Dad? He's not a nice person, and you are so nice and loving."

Evelyn looked at Bradley and replied, "I remember how he *used* to be…your father at one time was a very loving man who would do anything for me. He's changed over the years Bradley. I just keep hoping one day he realizes that we are more important to him than his career."

Bradley, confused by his mother's response, smiled and said, "Okay Mom, I hope you are right. I'll keep hoping too."

One day while Bradley was at home he was going through the family library and came across a book on dentistry. He grabbed the book and began to read it. He was so engrossed in the book he did not realize his mother was standing over him. Bradley turned around and saw his mother smiling at him. He looked up at his mom and asked who in the family was studying to be a dentist. Evelyn told Bradley her brother Jake was.

Bradley asked, "Your brother?"

With a mournful look in her eyes she told Bradley about her late brother. "Jake was my older brother—he *was* studying to be a dentist. He died in a car accident two months before his graduation. You remind me a lot of him you know, he was always reading and always kept to himself."

Sincerely,

Bradley smiled and asked his mother if she had more books of his. She looked at Bradley and showed him all of her brother's books from college and she even showed him the dental kit her parents bought him for college. Bradley's eyes lit up like a Christmas tree. He looked at his mother and said, "I am going to be a dentist just like my Uncle Jake!"

At this Evelyn smiled and said, "I am sure my brother would have liked that."

After that Bradley would come home from school, and after doing his homework he'd grab a snack and run straight to the family library to read more of his Uncle Jake's dental books and play with the dental kit's gadgets.

By the time Bradley was in the seventh grade James was running for governor. James invited the press to their wealthy family home for a press conference. He wanted to show the state of Tennessee a family that had traditional values and one that would represent the state of Tennessee. Evelyn was dressed in a designer dress, James wore a three-piece suit, and Bradley was dressed in a three-piece that was designed to match his father's.

The press conference was a great success. For most of it Bradley stayed quiet and observed the adults but he caught the attention of one of the reporters. They asked Bradley a question.

"Bradley, do you want to be in politics like your dad here and his father before him?"

Bradley smiled and answered, "No, I want to become a dentist like my Uncle Jake."

The reporter responded, "Well, that's bold and brave son, following a different path...at least it will keep you honest."

The other press members began to laugh at the reporter's response to Bradley's answer. James gave a giggle and looked over at Bradley with disapproval on his face.

After the press left James walked over to Bradley and slapped him across the face and said, "Don't ever fucking embarrass me like that again. A *fucking dentist*, really?"

Evelyn, furious at James, yelled, "DO NOT HIT MY SON! IF HE WANTS TO BE A DENTIST THAT'S HIS CHOICE! WHAT IS WRONG WITH YOU JAMES?! WHAT HAPPENED TO THE MAN I MARRIED?!"

She grabbed Bradley and brought him to her car. They needed a ride to de-stress...and talk. Evelyn began to cry and to apologize to Bradley for his father's behavior.

Bradley looked at his mom and said, "Don't worry about it. When I become a dentist I will charge him double."

Evelyn began to laugh. "I know what we can do to piss your father off."

Bradley giggled. "What?"

Evelyn smiled. "Let's go spend some of his money. After today we deserve a shopping spree."

Bradley agreed. When they arrived home carrying shopping bags from every store you could think of, James stood in the foyer to greet them.

Sincerely,

"I see you had a nice night of shopping. Did you enjoy yourselves?"

Bradley responded, "Actually Dad we did enjoy ourselves, we had a lot of laughs. Mom and I even shared a very large chocolate shake together."

James smiled at his son and said, "I am happy the two of you had a good time. I want to apologize for my behavior earlier Bradley. I should never have hit you, but you cannot ever embarrass me like that again."

Bradley put his head down. "Okay Dad."

Evelyn smiled at her husband for attempting to apologize to their son.

James then looked at his wife and Bradley and said, "All that shopping must have made you hungry. Let's go grab dinner and a movie."

Bradley looked over at his mother and said, "I am hungry how about you?"

Evelyn hugged James and suggested they go to the country club.

When Bradley was in ninth grade his father had already served a year and half as governor and he was planning on running for reelection. James's plans were to serve two terms as the governor of Tennessee and then to run for president of the United States.

One day while Bradley was at school one of the boys in his class began to tease him about his father being the governor. The boy's name was Justin Screen; he was the son of Senator Screen. Bradley would just look at Justin and smile and walk away. Justin would start to yell at Bradley, "What are you going to do, go cry to your loser daddy?" Bradley would just keep walking and not acknowledge Justin yelling at him. Justin continued to harass Bradley for the next few weeks. Each time Bradley would smile at him and walk away.

One particular day in gym class, Justin began to yell across the gym, "Hey Bradley, did you know your father is fucking his secretary?"

Bradley looked over at Justin and yelled, "Really? I thought he was fucking your drunk whore of a mother."

Everyone in the gym began to laugh at Bradley's retort. Justin's face turned beet red as he ran across the gym and punched him in the face. He just stood there for a minute and looked at Justin. Justin hit him again, only this time knocking him down to the ground where he proceeded to pummel him.

Bradley was unable to get Justin off him, so he grabbed Justin's arm and bit down as hard as he could. Justin began to scream. The more he screamed the harder Bradley bit. Bradley could taste blood in his mouth as he continued to bite down. A teacher came over to break up the fight, but the teacher was unaware that Bradley had Justin's arm in his mouth.

When the teacher pulled Justin off Bradley there was a sickening ripping sound as Justin's skin was torn off his arm. Justin dropped to the ground screaming. When the teacher looked over at Bradley he saw a large piece of skin hanging from his mouth. The teacher grabbed Bradley and brought him to the principal as Justin was rushed to the hospital for stitches.

Sincerely,

When Principal Lucy walked into the office she could not believe it was Bradley. She asked him what happened. When Bradley began to tell his side of the story she cut him short. She looked at him and said, "Regardless of what Justin said to you, it does not make it right. You bit him and now he is in the hospital getting stitches. I have to call your father."

When James arrived at the school he walked into Principal Lucy's office and asked what was so important that he had leave work. She told James of the incident between the two boys and declared that Bradley would be suspended indefinitely. She promised to recommend other schools for Bradley, but strongly suggested he be homeschooled.

James glared daggers at her, but simply said before leaving, "Have a good day."

The car ride home was silent, but when they arrived James began to yell, "WHAT THE FUCK WERE YOU THINKING?! YOU BIT A PIECE OF A KID'S ARM OFF—WHAT THE FUCK IS WRONG WITH YOU?!"

Bradley looked at his father and said, "Are you fucking your secretary?"

A little shocked and infuriated James began again. "WHAT THE FUCK DID YOU ASK ME?!"

Bradley simply asked him again. James left the room for a minute and when he returned, he was carrying a pair of pliers. He walked over to Bradley and threw him on the floor.

James sat on Bradley's stomach and yelled, "DO YOU HAVE ANY IDEA HOW MUCH YOU EM-

BARRASSED ME?! I AM THE FUCKING GOVERNOR AND MY FUCKING SON GETS THROWN OUT OF SCHOOL! THEN YOU HAVE THE BALLS TO ASK ME IF I AM FUCKING MY SECRETARY?!"

James demanded Bradley open his mouth. Bradley said, "NO!" James hit Bradley in the mouth with the pliers over and over again until he opened his mouth. James took the pliers and began to pull out Bradley's two front teeth. The first tooth he pulled out cracked in half.

Bradley began to scream. "STOP DAD, PLEASE STOP!"

James ignored his son's pleas to stop. James took the pliers and proceeded to rip the second front tooth out, tearing Bradley's gums. Then something began to happen to Bradley as he pleaded for his father to stop, something inside died. Hatred was building behind his fear. James proceeded to remove his bottom teeth, still ignoring his son's pleas to stop. Bradley could hear the sound of his teeth cracking in half. The pain of the pliers ripping his gums open was unbearable. Bradley continued screaming and begging for his father to stop.

When he finished he looked at Bradley and said, "See, you're not the only one who can be a dentist. Now let's see you try to fucking bite someone again you little shit. Now go clean up before your mother gets home."

Bradley went upstairs to his bedroom and looked into the mirror that was hanging over his dresser. When he opened his mouth he could not believe what his father had done to him. He ran to his bathroom and began to spit out all the blood that was in his mouth. As Bradley looked into the mirror he no longer saw the once loving child who tried to make his father happy. What he saw was a young man who had nothing but hate in his heart. He hated Justin for making him bite, he hated his father for torturing him, and he was upset with his mother for not being home to protect him.

Bradley continued to look into the mirror and his once hazel eyes were no longer green; the intensity of his glare turned them brown. As he saw the change in his eye color he looked at his reflection, mouthing along with his thoughts, *I Sincerely hate you, I hate you all. I will get revenge someday.* This was the moment Sincerely was born and Bradley faded away.

When Evelyn arrived home James approached her and said, "Your son was thrown out of school today for biting another child, I don't want you to worry about it. I made sure that your son will never bite another child again."

Evelyn looked at James with confusion. "What are you talking about? Where's Bradley? What did you do to him?"

Evelyn began to yell for Bradley. When he did not respond she ran to his room. As she opened his bedroom door she saw Bradley staring in the mirror. Bradley turned to look at his mother with tears in his eyes, but with a smile he showed his bloody mouth with his broken front tooth and the other teeth—nearly all of them—missing. Evelyn stood in shock. She

L.A. Brien

walked over to Bradley to hug him, but he turned a cold shoulder to her.

Steadily, he reached for a notepad and pen on his dresser and calmly wrote out a note. Before he was even finished, his mother was peering around his side to read it. The note asked her to leave his room and call a dentist to fix what her husband had done to him.

Evelyn began to cry. "Bradley, I am so sorry your father did this to you. Please believe I never thought he was capable of this."

Bradley turned stony eyes to his mother. Attempting to speak, he only managed some painful wet burbles, dripping a mix of blood and drool on the rug. His father had taken away any ability to enunciate, his very voice. Frustrated, he turned back to the notepad, violently ripped off the top page, and furiously scribbled out another message: *Get the Fuck out of my room and call a dentist.*

Evelyn, shocked by her son's response, ran down the stairs to her husband's office, grabbed the first object she saw, and threw it at James's head.

"WHAT THE HELL IS WRONG WITH YOU? YOU PULLED OUR CHILD'S TEETH OUT YOU SON OF A BITCH! I CANNOT DO THIS ANYMORE, I WANT A DIVORCE! I AM TAKING MY SON AND WE ARE LEAVING—"

James sat in his chair laughing. "Leave, I don't care. If you haven't heard yet I have been fucking my secretary. I will just tell everyone that you were having an affair. I am a governor who has strong moral values so I demanded a divorce."

Sincerely,

Evelyn responded, "Tell them whatever you want, I am moving back to my family estate and you can stay here and rot in hell for all I care."

Evelyn went upstairs to Bradley's room and told him to pack. They were no longer going to live in that house. Bradley hugged his mother and thanked her. When they arrived at Evelyn's family estate Bradley could not believe the size of the mansion his mother grew up in.

Evelyn looked at Bradley and said, "The one thing your father does not know was everything was left to me in trust so your father could never touch it. My parents never liked him and they wanted me to have a security blanket for the day I left your father."

Bradley just smiled.

The door to the mansion was opened by the housekeeper. "Welcome home Evelyn and Bradley."

Bradley just smiled, his mouth still throbbing and bleeding. Evelyn asked the housekeeper Mary to get Bradley some ice. Evelyn went into the kitchen to make a call. She came walking out with a smile on her face.

"Bradley, I have an old friend of mine coming over to look at your mouth. He is an oral surgeon. He was my brother Jake's best friend. While we wait for him to come over let me give you a tour of your new house."

Bradley smiled and gave a thumb's up. Okay.

While walking around the mansion Bradley could not believe the size of the library; it was twice as big as the one at his father's house. The next room they walked into was the game room with a pool table and a Pac-Man arcade game and pinball machines; it even had a movie theater and an indoor pool. Evelyn brought Bradley upstairs to the bedrooms and showed him Jake's old bedroom. Bradley asked—with a more polite note—if he could have it.

Evelyn smiled. "That would make me happy."

An hour later the doorbell rang and it was Will, Evelyn's late brother's best friend. He gave Evelyn a hug and extended his hand to Bradley. Bradley put his head down and extended his hand back. Will asked Jake to have a seat in the recliner. As he was looking in Bradley's mouth he gave a big sigh.

"Evelyn, could you come here for a minute? Your husband did one hell of job on this kid's mouth. He needs stitches, root canals, and surgery to remove the broken front tooth. This is going to take three or more months to fix all the damage. First things first, hand me my medical bag."

Will looked at Bradley. "I am going to give you some Novocain, then I am going to stitch up your gums." Bradley just nodded yes.

After Bradley was stitched up he thanked Will. Will smiled and said, "Don't thank me yet, we have a long way to go my friend."

Evelyn asked Will how long Bradley would have to go without teeth. Will explained to them both that the gums needed to heal before he could do anything. "What I can do is measure Bradley for temporary dentures. He will be able to eat without damaging the gums and no one should be able to tell he's wearing dentures."

Evelyn and Bradley agreed. Within a couple of weeks Bradley had his temporary dentures. His mother noticed that when Bradley was wearing the dentures he spoke with a slight lisp, but she never brought it to his attention. Evelyn told Bradley she had enrolled him in a private school, it would be a fresh start. Bradley was excited about going back to school, though was a little self-conscious about going back with dentures. He did not want people to know he had false teeth, even if it was temporary.

On Bradley's first day of school he was greeted by a girl named Sarah, who he called Tara. Tara was average height for a girl her age with straight auburn hair, and she had glasses and braces. Bradley smiled when he first met Tara and thought to himself she had an attractiveness about her. He found her cheerful greeting comforting. Tara gave him a tour of the school and introduced him to his new teachers and fellow classmates.

The first two weeks of school were just what Bradley needed. He was making friends and even participating in the gym class he once dreaded. Tara and Bradley became very close friends. The two of them would hang out after school and do their homework on the weekends together. She would hang out at Bradley's house watching movies in the theater or they'd challenge each other in a game of Pac-Man. Bradley never felt so happy in his life, he had someone he could call his best friend.

L.A. Brien

One day at school Tara and Bradley were sitting in the gym watching some of their friends playing basketball. One of the boys in Bradley's class, named Ross, asked him if he would like to play. Bradley was hesitant at first but agreed to play. The game was going well until Bradley went to shoot the ball in the hoop and the boy accidently hit Bradley in the mouth, knocking his dentures out on to the gym floor. Bradley could feel his heart pounding and heat rushing into his face as he saw his dentures lying there in front of everyone.

At first there was silence, then Ross pointed at the dentures on the floor and looked up at Bradley with most of his teeth missing. Ross began to laugh, saying, "What the fuck dude? What the fuck happened to your fucking mouth? Fucking freak."

Bradley could feel his face turn red from embarrassment as he ran over to where his dentures were lying. He grabbed them and ran out of the gym, but while he was running he could hear all the other boys laughing at him.

He could also hear Tara yelling for them to stop. "Stop your fucking laughing, it's not funny you assholes!"

Bradley ran into the bathroom and washed off his dentures, putting them back into his mouth. He then heard the bathroom door open. It was Tara who started to walk over to him.

She gave him hug and said, "I'm sorry they laughed at you. They are nothing but a bunch of jock assholes."

Sincerely,

Bradley just kept his head down and in a low voice said, "I didn't want anyone to know. I am working on getting my teeth fixed and this is only temporary. I am getting implants but I have to wait till my gums heal."

Tara looked at Bradley and said, "Take out your dentures." Bradley looked at her with a puzzled look, but did what she asked. Tara then walked up to him and began kissing him.

Bradley pulled back and said, "Are you trying to make me feel better?"

"No, I am trying to show you that to me it doesn't matter what's going on with your mouth. I like you know no matter what."

Bradley, not knowing what to do, thanked Tara for being a good friend.

Tara looked at him and said, "I would do anything for you, remember that." Bradley hugged her and said thank you. "Now let's get out of here." Tara said.

The next day in school Bradley was hoping that everyone would forget about the incident in the gym and life would go on as normal, but in high school kids never forget. When he arrived at his locker everything seemed to be going okay…until he opened it and about twenty boxes of denture glue fell out. Bradley started to pick the boxes off the floor as his classmates walked by, pointing and laughing.

Out of nowhere a student everyone called J.C. came over and started to help Bradley pick up the boxes. He looked at Bradley. "Don't let those assholes get to you. This week it will be you, next week it will be somebody else."

Bradley smiled and said, "I'm Bradley, thank you for helping me."

J.C. smiled. "I'm J.C. and no problem. Come on, I will walk you to class."

Unfortunately J.C. was wrong. His classmates continued to tease him; however, it didn't seem to faze him. He would simply smile and walk away. This kept most of them wondering why he did not let it get to him. What his classmates were unaware of was that he was remembering everyone who was teasing him and putting him down. He was making a list in his mind that someday his classmates would wish they were never on.

The one good thing that came out of the whole gym incident was that he now had a new friend, J.C. Both J.C. and Tara continued to hang out with Bradley after school and on the weekends. Over the course of the next few months his teeth were repaired and he no longer had to wear the dentures. When that day came the three friends went out dinner and a movie to celebrate. During dinner Bradley noticed that J.C. and Tara were becoming very close, he could see the two of them as a couple. Bradley did not want to feel like a third wheel so he told them that he was going to walk home and that he would see them tomorrow.

Bradley wanted to take a shortcut home so he decided to walk through Parmer Park. While walking through the park Bradley could not get over what a nice night it was. The sky was clear and the moon was full. He felt like the park was his, there was no one around. He was enjoying the walk through the park when he heard the sound of a bike coming in his direction. As the bike turned around the bend on the bike path, Bradley could see it was Justin Screen.

Bradley always imagined what he would do to Justin if he ever crossed paths with him. He imagined himself pulling out Justin's teeth like his father did to him. As Justin came closer to where Bradley was standing, his heart began to pound. He suddenly became enraged as he felt the only way to get rid of this feeling was to destroy Justin. Bradley's hands began to shake while the hate he felt for Justin began to grow overwhelming as Justin rode his bike closer to Bradley. Bradley saw a very large tree branch laying on the ground next him.

When Justin got close enough to Bradley he could hear Justin say, "Fucking freak!"

Bradley picked the tree branch up off the ground and hit Justin across the face, knocking him off his bike. Justin was on the ground. His nose was bleeding and he started to scream for help. Bradley picked up the tree branch, raised it up above his head, and brought it down hard, smashing Justin's skull.

As Justin lay on the ground lifeless Bradley looked at him, smiled, and said, "God that felt good."

Bradley dragged Justin's body under a tree and covered it with leaves. When Bradley got home he went upstairs to take a shower and change his clothes. He then walked into the kitchen where his mother was having a cup of tea. Evelyn was happy that Bradley was home and asked how his night was with his friends.

Bradley hugged his mother and said, "Mom, I had a good night; it turned out better than I thought." Then he smiled and continued, "Mom, any pie left? I had so much fun tonight I'm craving some homemade pie."

Evelyn hugged her son and smiled and said in a loving voice, "I am so lucky to have a son who is as wonderful as you."

Bradley in a joking manner said, "Yes, yes you are."

Bradley waited till his mother fell asleep to take her car and drive back to Parmer Park to move Justin's body. When he pulled up to the park he was looking around to make sure no one was around. He pulled some trash bags and a saw from the trunk of the car. He walked over to the body and said out loud, "Boy do I have some plans for you."

He began to cut up the body and divided the body parts into different bags. Then he drove to the next town and threw the bag that contained Justin's arms into a lake. The legs he threw into a pond, the torso he had propped up on tree stump in a wooded area. As for the head, he wanted to keep it.

The next morning when Bradley woke up his mother was watching the news. The news was covering the disappearance of a local boy, Justin Screen. Bradley asked his mother what was going on. Evelyn told Bradley that Justin was missing and his parents were looking for him.

Sincerely,

Bradley looked at his mother and said, "I'm sure they will find him. I hope he doesn't go to pieces." Evelyn then asked Bradley how he felt about Justin missing. Bradley replied, "I feel bad. I know we had our problems but I don't wish him any harm. The past is the past Mom. Besides if I never had that fight with Justin I would not have my two best friends. In my eyes our fight was the best thing that ever happened to me. I am happy now."

She smiled at him and told him how proud she was of him for making a bad situation into a positive one. She hugged him and told him she was going to work for a few hours and she'd be back later.

A couple weeks had gone by when the news came on that the torso of a male teen was found in a wooded area on a tree stump. "Investigators are running a DNA test. The police will not say if it belonged to the missing boy Justin Screen."

Evelyn called Bradley into the family room. "Bradley, the police found the torso of a young male. If you are going out with your friends please be careful. If you want to go to the movies or the mall you need to have myself or your friends' parents take you. It's not safe right now; we have no idea what kind of sick person did this. I need to know you are safe, do you understand me?"

Bradley smiled at his mom and said, "Okay Mom, no problem."

As Evelyn headed towards the kitchen to get her keys for work she began talking to herself. "What kind of sick person would do such a thing? Please

122

Lord, keep my son safe." Evelyn walked out of the house and headed to work.

Later that day Bradley told Mary the house-keeper that he would be in his uncle's old work shed, working on his science project which was due in a week. He told her he did not want to be disturbed. Mary made him a lunch and some drinks to take with him in case he got hungry. The work shed was a small house set on the back of the property. It had a couch, a bookcase, a table and chairs and fridge. When Bradley entered the work shed he put his lunch in the fridge and put one of the drinks on the table.

He then opened a small box which contained his dentures. Bradley then placed a black trash bag on the table which contained Justin's head. Bradley picked up Justin's head by the hair and said, "Now let's see what a good dentist I will become."

Bradley began to remove Justin's teeth one by one. Then he removed the teeth from his old dentures. Bradley took Justin's teeth and carefully placed them into his dentures. He started laughing looking at Justin's head, saying out loud, "Holy shit...Justin, I never realized how big your teeth were."

Bradley, realizing how big they actually were, decided to use porcelain glue on the teeth to keep them in place. But due to the size of Justin's teeth they appeared crooked and too big for the dentures. Bradley picked up the dentures and placed them in his mouth— it made an impressive mouthful what with his new implants—and looked into a mirror that was hanging on the wall.

As he was staring at his reflection Evelyn entered the work shed. When she went to ask Bradley a question he turned around, wearing the dentures. Evelyn stood staring at her son with the second set of teeth bulging out of his mouth. She just froze as she saw Justin's decomposing head on the table. She began to shake uncontrollably and tears began to pour down her face.

Bradley, dentures still in his mouth, said, "What's wrong mother?"

Evelyn tried to scream but nothing would come out. She just stood shaking before she eventually passed out from fear. Bradley took the dentures out and placed them in the black trash bag along with Justin's head. He took the bag and threw it into an old well that was on the property. Bradley called Mary and told her to dial 911.

When Evelyn woke up she was in the hospital. She was very confused and scared, hoping it was all a nightmare. The doctors tried talking to her but she would not say a word. She stared at the wall in her room. The doctors came to inform her that her son was there to see her. When he approached the bed Evelyn sat up. She began rocking back and forth. As Bradley got closer to the bed she began yelling, "YOU ARE SINCERELY NOT MY SON! YOU ARE SINCERELY NOT MY SON! YOU ARE SINCERELY NOT MY SON!"

Bradley leaned over and whispered in her ear, "Yes Mother, I am Sincerely."

Evelyn began to scream as tears poured down her face.

The doctor ran back into the room and asked what happened. Bradley said, "I don't know she just started screaming." The doctor asked Bradley to leave, feeling it necessary to sedate Evelyn.

Six months later Evelyn returned home. She was heavily medicated and spent most of her time in her room. Bradley would visit his mother in her room on a daily basis and each time she would simply start to rock back and forth and repeat, "You are Sincerely, not my son." And over the next few years Evelyn's condition remained the same.

Bradley graduated magna cum laude in his high school class. The day of his graduation Bradley was giving a speech and as he was speaking he looked up into the audience and saw a man standing in the entranceway. It was his father. He turned, looking directly at his father, while proclaiming his thanks to his mother for the amazing job she did raising him and talking about how she taught him values and how to achieve goals in life.

He took a deep breath and said, "Due to her health she was unable to attend today's graduation. But I know she is at home thinking of me." When Bradley looked up again he saw his father walk out the door. That was one of the last times he ever saw the man.

Bradley went on to college and became a dentist. One night while he was out grabbing a bite to eat after being in class he heard a familiar voice.

Sincerely,

"Hey Bradley, how are you?" He turned around and it was Ross from high school.

Bradley replied, "Hey how are you? I was hoping to run into you someday."

Back To Present Day

After Bradley left Rhode Island he headed back to Tennessee to pay a visit to his estranged father. When he arrived at his father's house the man was in his bed soundly asleep. Bradley tapped him on the head before whispering, "Wake up Father."

James's eyes opened up abruptly, his eyes shifting around to shake the sleepiness off as he saw his son Bradley standing before him. He tried to get up but soon realized he had been tied sturdily to the bedposts. James began to yell. "What are you doing?! Untie me right now!"

Bradley just smiled at his father. "Father it's been so long...I thought it was time we had a little chat."

James roared, "UNTIE ME RIGHT NOW! WHEN I AM UNTIED I WILL TALK TO YOU!"

Bradley began to laugh. "Really Father, you act like I don't know you. You are not a man of your word, never have been."

His father responded, "What do you want?"

Bradley started his long awaited monologue. "Since we have not spoken in so many years, I thought I would fill you in on the parts of my life you've missed, as well as my accomplishments. To begin...I did become a dentist, and a very successful one at that. You could say I have become quite famous even."

James interrupted his son's speech. "What, are we upset that I didn't support your career choice? Are you looking for me to apologize for what I did to you? What do you want Bradley?"

Bradley shook his head. "Oh Father, still playing the politician. No, I am here to thank you. Ripping the teeth out of my mouth was the best thing that ever happened. You made me the man I am today. Now, let me go back to what I was trying to say shall we?

"I wanted to tell you father, not only am I famous now...but I actually met quite the woman. Her name is Lisa—or Lou, most people call her Lou—I think I prefer that. Anyways, she is the total opposite of who I am. She's kind, she cares about people." He paused. "She prays, *a lot*." He began to chuckle. "It's too bad. I am going to have to kill her."

James pulled frantically at the ropes as he bellowed, "Bradley, if you care so much for this girl why would you want to hurt her?!"

Bradley let out a belly laugh. "Oh my God, really. Giving me advice about not hurting people. Now, that's funny. You still don't get it, let me show you. I will be back in a minute."

When Bradley left the room James was writhing on the bed, unsuccessfully yanking against the restraints. Within a few moments Bradley came walking back into his father's room, carrying the housekeeper's head in his hand. Her teeth had been removed.

Sincerely,

James began to shriek. "WHY?! PLEASE UNTIE ME!"

Bradley threw the head on the floor. "Father you can scream and shout all you want, cry even. I don't care. You will be no different from any other person I have come in contact with."

James with tears pouring down his face said to his son, "What are you talking about?"

Bradley began to smile at his father. "Do you ever read the paper? I know you used to. Father I am the serial killer, Sincerely."

James began to shake his head with disbelief as the tears continued rolling down his face. "No, you're my son."

Bradley retorted with no emotion on his face, "Father, I have not been your son in a very long time. Not that it mattered, you were dead to me the night you did what you did. I don't know how much more time I have left with my girl Lou. Did I mention she is a private investigator? She's pretty close to figuring out who I am...so I may end up in jail. Or dead, but I plan to buy myself some more time and leave the country for a while.

"Enough of that, I am to share my life with you now. Like how things should be. Let me begin, the clock is ticking." He motioned mockingly to the watch on his wrist.

"Obviously, Justin was my first. It really wasn't my best work, but I was only fifteen. Ross was my first *success*...but my second kill. I met up with him after graduation—the pussy acted like nothing had

128

ever happened in high school. I went along with it. I invited him over to my work shed at mother's house. We had a few drinks—well, he *thought* I was drinking. It was only water, I was drinking water—my acting skills are great too you know. The fucker was so intoxicated, it was too easy. I knocked him out and tied him up and laid him on the floor. I threw a cup of water on him to wake him up though; otherwise it would have been no fun. When he finally came to, I very nicely explained I was going to remove all of his teeth and cut off his head and leave it where *everyone* could see. I grabbed my pliers and ripped out every single one of the fucker's teeth."

Bradley paused, looking quite proud of himself before continuing, "Let me tell you Father, the screams were *curdling*! Did I scream that loud when you ripped my teeth out of my face Father? Oh never mind, you don't have to answer. Eventually, I had to put the poor thing out of his misery. As promised there was a great reveal where I placed his decapitated shit-brain head on a bike path...signed, Sincerely. At first I was unsure what to do with the teeth you know, then it came me to engrave the teeth of my victims and place them into my patients. Who would know?!" he said proudly. "This way they can live on, but in a better person's body. So... if you think about it I have given all of them a second chance. On occasion you get the people who deserve to be placed in hell, so the teeth belonging to those I implant into prisoners throughout the country. I know what you're thinking—they're dead, it doesn't matter. But in my mind it's my way of punishing them after death."

James just stared at his son with fear in his eyes. He was afraid to speak but he did anyway. "Bradley I can get you help…you will never see a prison."

At this Bradley laughed. "Oh, Father you haven't changed, still trying to beat the system…even for your serial killer son. The answer is no, I don't want your help. I'm not even going to kill you. I'm going to make you remember me, and what you did to me, for the rest of your life."

Bradley pulled a pair of pliers out of his coat as he leaned over his father and said, "This will only hurt for a little while. Open wide."

James was finally able to let out a scream. Bradley pried his father's mouth opened and began to laugh. Despite his father's cries and squirming he pulled out every one of his father's teeth. James was screaming and begging for him to stop. James began shaking, the blood choking him until he could scream no longer.

Bradley could hear the blood gurgling in the back of his throat. He sat his father up in the bed and gently untied the restraints. He told him that he should get rid of the maid's body; he wouldn't want to be charged for murder. Bradley looked at his father one last time before leaving him there.

"Maybe we should get together again sometime Father."

James did not answer, he did not move. He sat in the bed crying hysterically.

Chapter 7

TENNESSEE

When Lou and Marianne landed in Tennessee they were warmly greeted by Joanne. Joanne was happy to see her old friends, but not under these circumstances.

She hugged her friends before saying, "My car is outside. I found a hotel for us in Belle Meade. We can stay there." When they got into the car Joanne started telling them about her friend Craig, a police officer that investigated Bradley when he was a teenager.

Lou looked at Joanne with confusion. "What do you mean a teenager? How long has this sick fuck been killing people?"

Sincerely,

Joanne looked at Lou and replied, "I will let my friend Craig tell you. Let's get to the hotel and get something to eat."

Marianne interjected, "I could go for a cold beer right now."

Lou laughed and replied, "I could go for a beer too."

After checking into the hotel the three ladies found a restaurant close by and ordered a round of beers and appetizers. When they were on their second round, a man in his early sixties about six feet tall with a rugged build and salt and pepper hair approached the table carrying a file. Joanne stood up and greeted the man. She introduced her friend Craig and Lou smiled and extended her hand.

"Nice to meet you Craig, I'm Lou. Jo filled us in about you on the ride over."

Marianne gave a polite wave and introduced herself before smiling and saying, "I really hope you have something we can use. I need this to be over so I can get back to my family."

Craig sat down at the table, sighed and replied, "I hope I do too." Craig ordered a scotch on the rocks and handed Lou a file. "Joanne filled me in on what's been going on. I would bet my life that it's Bradley. Only in this here case, he didn't leave a head. He left a torso, without one. I truly believe Justin was his first kill." Craig told the ladies about the reported altercation between Bradley and Justin as classmates and how Justin went missing shortly after that. He explained the torso of the boy's body was found in a wooded area, and how the head was never found.

He went on to tell the three women on how he met Bradley. "When I was investigating Justin's disappearance, Bradley's name had come up several times with a few of the kids and the principal at school. I was told about a violent confrontation between the two boys. At the time I didn't think a fourteen-year-old boy would be responsible for such a heinous crime. I decided to pay the boy a visit and when I arrived his mother Evelyn answered the door with a warm welcome, she was a very kind woman. I introduced myself and she invited me in, and she asked why I was there. I had to explain I was interviewing kids who might have known Justin or might offer some clue as to what happened."

Craig paused to take a sip of his drink before continuing. "I recall that the boy's mother just put her head down before saying that I must have heard about the fight between the two boys. I admitted that I had but offered an excuse, stating I only wanted to ask the kids if they had seen anyone driving around the schools or the parks. Evelyn called for her son, introduced us. Bradley seemed polite enough when I told him I was a detective investigating the murder of Justin Screen. He had an odd calm but cold demeanor and agreed to answer any questions about Justin but was quite forward but defensive, asking me why I would want to ask *him* about Justin's murder. I remember him saying, 'It's not like we're friends. I feel bad about what happened to him, but he was not the nicest person in the world.'

Sincerely,

"I was surprised by Bradley's answer, and asked him if he thought Justin deserved being murdered. At this, the boy smiled strangely, before saying 'No one deserves to be murdered, but I am not going to lose sleep over someone who made my life a living hell in school. I hope you catch the person who did this, my friends and I don't feel safe going out and if we do we are asking our parents to drive us and pick us up.'

"I continued my questioning, and asked where he was on the night of Justin's murder. At that the boy's mother interjected seemingly upset, and telling me I should leave. But the boy answered anyways. He told me he was out with his friends that night, enjoyed pie with his mother before retiring to bed. The boy asked if I had any more questions. I didn't at the time, but I can tell you something in my gut, in my very being told me I was in the right place."

At this Lou quickly asked, "Did you check his alibi?"

Craig answered, "Of course I checked his alibi. He told…the truth."

Lou becoming rather impatient asked, "Then why did you think it was him?"

With a look of defeat Craig ruefully answered, "My gut said it was this kid. That kid was not wired right, something was missing. He had no empathy towards a person he knew who was just murdered. Later on I heard his mother had a nervous breakdown, she has never been the same. Bradley went off to college. That was the last I heard for a long time. Then when I

134

began to hear about the Sincerely cases, I knew it had to be Bradley. I just couldn't prove it."

Lou in an understanding voice asked Craig, "Does Bradley's mother still live in the same house?"

Craig answered, "Yes, she does. From what I understand her housekeeper Maria lives with her."

Lou smiled. "Great, I guess we are going to start with Bradley's mother."

Marianne looking concerned asked, "What if Bradley is there?! Lou we don't even have a gun on us! We have no protection, what if he tries to come after us?"

At this Craig laughed. "Marianne you have nothing to worry about, I will give you a handgun. If you don't mind I would like to go with you to question Bradley's mother."

Marianne feeling more relaxed answered, "Yes, I think you should come."

Lou laughed. "Well, Craig, my deputy has spoken."

The following morning the ladies woke up to a loud knock on the door. It was Craig.

"Good morning ladies," he said as he walked in quickly, "I brought coffee and donuts. Joanne is waiting in the car downstairs."

Lou looked at Craig and said, "Holy shit, I thought I was an early bird. We will meet you downstairs, give us fifteen minutes." Craig grabbed a donut and his coffee and headed back downstairs. Lou went to the bathroom and as she was getting ready she looked in the mirror and prayed silently for God to keep her and her friends safe.

When they arrived at Bradley's childhood home the four of them could not believe that a serial killer grew up in such a mansion. When they went to leave the car Joanne told Lou she would be staying behind. If they needed her medical opinion on something she would offer it. Craig rang the doorbell and Maria the housekeeper answered.

"Hello, how can I help you?" Craig showed his badge and said he would like to meet with Evelyn. Maria asked, "May I ask what this is regarding?"

Craig replied, "No, I need to speak to Evelyn myself."

Maria seemed confused, but obliged. "Okay, but she doesn't speak. She has not spoken in years. She suffered from a nervous breakdown many years ago."

Lou chimed in. "Hello, my name is Lou. I am fully aware and understand that she has some mental health issues, but I only need a few minutes of her time." Maria let the three of them in the house and led them to Evelyn's room.

When they entered the room they saw an older attractive woman sitting at a desk. She was writing in what looked to be a scrapbook. As Lou looked around the room she noticed photos of Bradley when he was a young child. Some photos were of Bradley, some of his childhood friends. Craig stood there staring at Evelyn. He could not believe that was the same woman he had met with years ago. Maria introduced Craig and Lou to

Evelyn. She kept her head down and continued to write.

Craig looked at Lou and said, "I think it might have been a mistake coming here. She doesn't even know what planet she is on."

Marianne looked at Lou and said, "I don't think this was a good idea either Lou, this poor woman is broken."

Lou began to get angry at the two of them for giving up so quickly. Lou approached Evelyn and asked, "What are you putting in your scrapbook?"

Evelyn simply continued to write.

As Lou leaned forward to look at the scrapbook, she noticed it was all articles about Sincerely. Evelyn was repeatedly writing, "YOU ARE SINCERELY, NOT MY SON" over and over again. When Evelyn turned the page to continue, Lou noticed the article about her assault by Jack Coral. The article had a picture of Lou and a picture of Jack. Perplexed, Lou turned to look at Marianne. Evelyn looked at the picture and then looked at Lou again. Lou began to walk towards Marianne. Just then Evelyn grabbed her by the arm. Lou turned back towards her and she began to write, "SINCERELY IS MY SON, SINCERELY IS MY SON."

Lou looked at her and said, "I want to stop your son from hurting anymore people, how can I do that?"

Evelyn began to write, "KILL HIM!! KILL HIM!!! HE IS EVIL. HE IS ALWAYS WATCHING ME." Lou began to look around the room. Just then she spotted a small video camera in the far corner of the room.

Marianne grabbed one of the pictures and said, "Lou, this looks like a younger version of the woman we saw at the secondhand store in Texas."

Lou looked closely. "That's Sarah, Jack's wife. Oh my God, she's the one who set me up. She knows Sincerely."

Lou walked over to the camera and held up the picture of Sarah, Bradley, and Jack to it. She stuck her middle finger up at the camera and said, "I'm coming for you, I know who you are."

Craig grabbed Lou and Marianne and headed towards the door. Maria was standing by the door waiting to open it for the departing guests. Lou stopped and asked Maria if she knew who the people in the picture were.

Maria smiled. "Of course I do, it's Bradley, J.C., and Sara. Bradley had some dental work done and he couldn't pronounce certain words. Chiefly, he would call Sarah 'Tara.'" Lou thanked Maria and the three of them left the house.

When they reached the car where Joanne was waiting Craig leaned under the car seat and pulled out a pint of whiskey. He took a swig and said, "You ladies need to head back home. He knows you were in his house and he now knows we know his identity." Joanne was also concerned for her friends and began to call the airlines to get them back to Rhode Island.

Just then Lou's cellphone rang. It was her father. "Hi Pop, how are you?" Lou asked.

L.A. Brien

The voice on the other end was not her father's. It was Sincerely.

"SINCE YOU WANTED TO VISIT MY MOTHER, I THOUGHT IT ONLY APPROPRIATE TO VISIT YOUR FATHER! I HOPE YOU MAKE IT BACK TO RHODE ISLAND IN TIME! UNTIL THEN...DADDY AND I ARE GOING TO GET TO KNOW EACH OTHER VERY WELL!"

Lou screamed violently into the phone, "LEAVE MY FATHER ALONE! WHAT DO YOU WANT?!"

Sincerely calmly replied, "Your head."

"Okay. Tell me where you want to meet. If I agree to meet you, you let my father go?"

Seeming pleased with himself and Lou's answer, he answered back, "Agreed. Since I have taken a liking to your hometown of Pawtucket... meet us at the Slater Mill. The clock is ticking. We will meet in five hours." With that he hung up, leaving Lou frantic.

On the other side of the call Sincerely looked at Michael and said, "Your daughter has offered me her head...for your freedom. She amazes me; she actually cares about people and cares so little about herself. Well Daddy, guess you brought our girl up right. She will be my best trophy yet."

Michael was badly beaten and tied to a chair with his mouth duct taped. He could only sit silently knowing Sincerely was right, tears streaming down and rolling over his taped face.

Chapter 8

THE MEETING OF GOOD AND EVIL

While on the plane ride back home Lou had to explain to Marianne that she would not be going with her. She explained that her friendship meant more to her than anything. She began apologizing for ever putting her in this situation.

Marianne with tears in her eyes asked, "Why are you saying all these things to me?"

Lou told her about the agreement she made with Sincerely.

Marianne broke down and started crying. "I am going with you, we are finishing this together. If Sincerely kills you my family is still in danger. He is going to have to kill the both of us together. I will not have my family harmed, we need to end this."

Lou, knowing her friend was right, agreed. When the plane arrived she and Marianne headed back to her home. She grabbed her mace and Bella's gun and got into her car and drove to Slater Mill to meet Sincerely.

As they pulled up Lou noticed that only one of three of the old mills had a light on inside. She told Marianne to stay close to her while placing the gun in the back of her pants and handed Marianne the mace. As they entered the mill her heart was pounding so fiercely she thought it was going to burst out of her chest.

When they entered the machine shop of Slater Mill she saw her father tied to an old wooden chair that stood next to an old coal stove. As she went to approach her father Sincerely walked out from behind one of the many spinning machines once used to make cotton. Lou was shocked to see a familiar face: her dentist Dr. Tamin.

With a gruesome smile on his face he said, "We meet again. I see you don't follow instruction very well. Why is Marianne with you?"

She stood in disbelief, not knowing what to say.

Sincerely began to laugh. "Is that how you greet your dentist?"

Marianne suddenly yelled, "Are you fucking kidding me, he's the one who fixed your teeth?!"

Lou looked at him with her eyes filled with rage. "Let my father go and you can have me!"

Sincerely stood and stared at her for a moment and with a grin he asked, "How are your teeth?" Surprised by the question she stood and stared without answering. He asked again, this time more violently. "*I said,* how are your teeth?!"

"My damn teeth are fine," she answered in disgust.

He began to smile and relaxed his tone. "I'm glad, because I put a lot of work into that mouth, not to mention your friend Bella."

It took a moment for her to realize what he meant—this man put her one of best friend's teeth in her mouth! She could feel herself beginning to dizzily unravel. She glanced around the room quickly and saw a pair old rusty pliers resting on a nearby table. She quickly shifted her body and grabbed them.

"Fuck you!" Lou began yanking out the teeth that Sincerely put in her. She screamed as she was pulling the teeth out. She tore her gums open and blood was dripping from her mouth.

Marianne yelled, "STOP, STOP IT!!"

Michael was screaming through the duct tape as he was trying to free himself to save his daughter. Sincerely stared at Lou with absolute rage in his eyes, upset that she just destroyed his work. At that moment he grabbed a knife and held it over her father and said loudly, "Say goodbye!!"

She started to run toward her father as Marianne grabbed the gun from the waistband of her pants. She threw herself over her father just as the knife was ready to pierce him, plunging into her back instead.

She dropped to the floor as Marianne yelled, "Fuck you, you son of a bitch!!" firing three shots into Sincerely.

When he dropped to the ground Marianne untied Michael. He grabbed his daughter and held her tight. "Please don't leave me kid, I love you," he said. Marianne called the police and asked for a rescue.

Chapter 9

THE HEALING TIME

ou stood in the mirror one morning a few months later, looking at the scars on her body left there from Sincerely and his friend Jack Coral, and she thanked God for surviving her ordeal. As she was getting ready to go to the prison to see Sincerely for one last time, she had a sense of relief knowing that Jack Coral received twenty-five years for attempted murder. Sarah received fifteen years for conspiracy to commit murder, and Bradley "Sincerely" received life without the possibility of parole.

When she arrived at the prison her friend Scott escorted her to a room where the visit would take place. As she walked in she saw Sincerely with his hands and feet cuffed. Scott told her he would be right outside the door if she needed anything.

Sincerely smiled at her before saying, "I am so glad you came."

"I was curious about what you had to say to me." The first thing he asked was if she had her teeth fixed. She rolled her eyes and answered that she had. He told her he was disappointed that she wrecked all of his hard work. She responded by saying, "You put my friend's teeth in my mouth. Of course I am going to get rid of it you sick fuck. Is that all you wanted to ask me, if I got my teeth fixed?"

"No, I have a question for you. When you stand there at night in front of your crucifix, do you ever for pray me?"

Lou, puzzled by his question, answered, "Yes, I pray God has mercy on your soul."

Sincerely looked surprised before asking, "Why? I am everything you're not. I could care less if someone lives or dies. Do you think I care about any one of my victims, including your friend Bella? I did her a favor, she was dying anyway. Her husband was a patient of mine and told me all about her health issues. I put that bitch out of her misery."

Lou stood up and said, "You're not God. Only he decides who lives and who dies."

With a smug look on his face he responded, "Really? Maybe I am God. I took many lives and I decided to take them. Not your God. Are you still going to pray for me now?"

Lou got up and started walking towards the door, before turning and answering, "Yes...I pray you go to hell."

Sincerely,

As she walked out the door Sincerely smiled and said, "That's my girl."

When she pulled up to her new lake house in Coventry her father was standing in the driveway. He was holding a pizza and a six-pack of beer. Lou and her father sat on the dock drinking beers, looking at the beautiful view.

Just then her cellphone began to ring. She answered and it was her old friend Tracy, who worked for the FBI. She asked Lou if she would look over a case for her.

Lou sighed deeply before looking over to her father and asking, "Are you ready to work together again Pop?"

The End

About the Author

I would like to introduce myself to my readers. My name is L.A. Brien. I was born and raised in Pawtucket, a city in the small state of Rhode Island. I find writing about myself the more challenging part of writing a book. What I will tell you is that I am new to the world of writing and never imagined in my life that I would have a book published. Growing up I always had an overactive imagination that carried into my adult life. Some of my friends have always told me I should write a book. I always said, "I don't think so!" Then something happened, the little thing called life, and I felt I needed to find an outlet, and I found it in writing. Enjoy!